RAIN
REIGN

RAIN
REIGN

Ann M. Martin

Feiwel and Friends
New York

A Feiwel and Friends Book
An Imprint of Macmillan

Feiwel and Friends books may be purchased for business or promotional use. For information on bulk purchases, please contact the Macmillan Corporate and Premium Sales Department at (800) 221-7945 x5442 or by e-mail at specialmarkets@ macmillan.com.

Library of Congress Cataloging-in-Publication Data Available

ISBN: 978-0-312-64300-3 (hardcover) / 978-1-250-06423-3 (ebook)

Book design by Ashley Halsey

Feiwel and Friends logo designed by Filomena Tuosto

First Edition: 2014

10

mackids.com

In memory of sweet Sadie,
March 11, 1998–October 7, 2013

I

The First Part

1
Who I Am—
A Girl Named
Rose (Rows)

I am Rose Howard and my first name has a homonym. To be accurate, it has a *homophone*, which is a word that's pronounced the same as another word but spelled differently. My homophone name is Rows.

Most people say *homonym* when they mean *homophone*. My teacher, Mrs. Kushel, says this is a common mistake.

"What's the difference between making a mistake and breaking a rule?" I want to know.

"Making a mistake is accidental. Breaking a rule is deliberate."

"But if—" I start to say.

Mrs. Kushel rushes on. "It's all right to say 'homonym' when we mean 'homophone.' That's called a colloquialism."

" 'Breaking' has a homonym," I tell her. " 'Braking.' "

I like homonyms a lot. And I like words. Rules and numbers too. Here is the order in which I like these things:

1. Words (especially homonyms)
2. Rules
3. Numbers (especially prime numbers)

I'm going to tell you a story. It's a true story, which makes it a piece of nonfiction.

This is how you tell a story: First you introduce the main character. I'm writing this story about me, so I am the main character.

My first name has a homonym, and I gave my dog a homonym name too. Her name is Rain, which is special because it has two homonyms—rein and reign. I will write more about Rain in Chapter Two. Chapter Two will be called "My Dog, Rain (Reign, Rein)."

Something important about the word *write* is that it has *three* homonyms—right, rite, and wright. That's the only group of four homonyms I've thought of. If I ever think of another four-homonym group, it will be a red-letter day.

I live with my father, Wesley Howard, and neither of his names has a homonym.

From our porch you can see our front yard and our driveway and our road, which is called Hud Road. *Road* has two homonyms—rowed and rode. On the other side (sighed) of the road is a little forest, and through the trees you can see the New York Thruway. The word *see* has a homonym—sea. But even better, *sees* has two homonyms—seas and seize.

I'm in fifth grade at Hatford Elementary. There's only one elementary school in Hatford, New York, and only one fifth-grade classroom in the school, and I'm in it. Most of my classmates are ten years old or about to turn eleven. I'm almost twelve because no one is sure what to do with me in school. I've stayed back for two semesters, which is a total of one year. ($1/2 + 1/2 = 1$.)

Some of the things I get teased about are following the rules and always talking about homonyms. Mrs. Leibler is my aide and she sits with me in Mrs. Kushel's room. She sits in an adult-size chair next to my fifth-grade-size chair and rests her hand on my arm when I blurt something out in the middle of math. Or, if I whap myself in the head and start to cry, she'll say, "Rose, do you need to step into the hall for a moment?"

Mrs. Leibler tells me that there are things worth talking about besides homonyms and rules and prime numbers. She encourages me to think up conversation starters. Some conversation starters about me that do not have anything to do with homonyms or rules or prime numbers are:

I live in a house that faces northeast. (After I say that, I ask the person I'm trying to have a conversation with, "And which direction does *your* house face?")

Down the road, 0.7 miles from my house is the J & R Garage, where my father sometimes works as a mechanic, and 0.1 miles farther along is a bar called The Luck of the Irish, where my father goes after work. There is nothing between my house and the J & R Garage except trees and the road. (Tell me some things about *your* neighborhood.)

I have an uncle named Weldon, who is my father's younger brother. (And who else is in *your* family?)

My official diagnosis is high-functioning autism, which some people call Asperger's syndrome. (Do *you* have a diagnosis?)

I will finish up this part of my introduction by telling you that my mother does not live with my father and me. She ran away from our family when I was two. Therefore, the people living in my house are my father and me. The dog living in our house is Rain. Uncle Weldon lives 3.4 miles away on the other side of Hatford.

The next part of my introduction is the setting of my story. I've already told you my geographic location— Hud Road in Hatford, New York. The historical moment in time in which this story begins is October of my year in fifth grade.

Now I will tell you something troubling about fifth grade. It isn't as troubling as what happens later in the story when my father lets Rain outside during a hurricane, but it is still troubling. For the first time in my life I'm being sent home with weekly progress reports that I have to give to my father. The reports are written by Mrs. Leibler and read and signed by Mrs. Kushel, which is my teachers' way of saying that they're in agreement about my behavior. The reports list all of my notable behaviors for Monday through Friday. Some of the comments are nice, such as the ones about when I participate appropriately in a classroom discussion. But most of the comments make my father slam the reports onto the table and say, "Rose, for god's sake, keep your mouth closed when you think of a homonym," or, "Do you see any of the other kids clapping their hands over their ears and screaming when they hear the fire alarm?"

In the last report Mrs. Leibler and Mrs. Kushel asked my father to schedule monthly meetings with them. Now he's supposed to go to Hatford Elementary on the third Friday of every month at 3:45 p.m. to discuss me. This is what he said when he read that: "I don't have time for meetings. This is way too much trouble, Rose. Why do you *do* these things?" He said that at 3:48 p.m. on a Friday when there was no work for him at the J & R Garage.

Uncle Weldon heard about the monthly meetings on October 3rd at 8:10 in the evening when he was visiting my father and Rain and me.

My father was standing at the front door, holding the letter in his hand and gazing out at the trees and the darkness. "These meetings are crap," he said.

Uncle Weldon, who was sitting at the Formica kitchen table with me, looked at my father from under his eyelashes and said, "I could go, if you want." Uncle Weldon has a very soft voice.

My father whipped around and pointed his finger at Weldon. "No! Rose is my responsibility. I can take care of things."

Weldon lowered his head and didn't answer. But when my father turned around so that he was facing outside again, my uncle held up two crossed fingers, which was his signal to me that everything would be all right (write, rite, wright). I held up my fingers too (two, to), and we each touched our hearts with them.

After that, Rain came into the kitchen and sat on my feet for a while.

Then my uncle left.

Then my father crumpled the letter from Mrs. Leibler and Mrs. Kushel and tossed it into the yard.

That is the end of the introduction to me.

2

My Dog, Rain
(Reign, Rein)

The next character in my true story is Rain. A character doesn't have to be a human being; a character can be an animal, such as a dog named Rain.

Rain weighs 23 pounds. This is how you weigh a dog: You stand on the scales and weigh yourself. Then you pick up the dog and weigh yourself and the dog together. Then you subtract your weight from the weight of you and the dog together, and that's how much the dog weighs.

(Weigh and way are homonyms.)

Rain's back is 18 inches long. From the tip of her nose to the tip of her tail she's 34 inches long.

Rain's fur is mostly yellow. Seven of her toes are white—two on her right front paw, one on her left front paw, three on her right back paw, and one on her left back paw. Her right ear has brown speckles on it. Her fur is short. Uncle Weldon says she looks sort of like a yellow Labrador retriever. Since a female purebred yellow Lab should weigh 55–70 pounds, Rain is probably not a purebred yellow Lab.

When Rain and I are at home alone together, we sit inside or on the front porch and Rain puts one (won) of her front feet (feat) in (inn) my lap. I rub her toes (tows), and she gazes into my blue (blew) eyes with her eyes, which are the color of a chocolate bar. After a while, she starts to fall asleep. Her brown eyes squint shut until they're completely closed. At bedtime she crawls under the covers with me. If I wake up during the night, I find that Rain has smashed her body against mine and rested her head across my neck.

Rain's breath smells like dog food.

Rain has lived with us for 11 months, which is almost one year. I will tell you more about the night my father brought her home in another chapter, Chapter Five, which will be called "When We Got Rain."

Rain and I have routines. We like routines. Rain stays at home alone on weekdays while I'm at Hatford Elementary and my father is at his job at the J & R Garage.

When there isn't any work for my father at the J & R Garage, he usually goes to The Luck of the Irish where he drinks beer and watches television. One way or the other, he isn't at home. Rain stays in the house by herself. At 2:42 when school ends, Uncle Weldon picks me up. Then he drives me home. He drops me off between 2:58 and 3:01. Rain and I sit on the porch for a while and I rub her toes. Then we take a walk. Then I do my homework. Then I start dinner for my father and me. Then I feed Rain.

What Rain eats is My Pet dog food from a can—half a can in the morning and half a can in the evening—mixed with My Pet dry food. When my father first brought Rain home he said she didn't need wet food, which is more expensive than dry food, but I said that dogs in the wild eat meat, and my father said, "You're right, Rose."

After Rain's dinner we wait for my father to come home. If he's been at The Luck of the Irish all day, he might not be in a good mood. Or he might be in a very good mood. If he's been working at the J & R Garage, he might not be in a good mood. Or he might be in no particular mood.

Rain is smart. She never goes near my father right away. She stands in the doorway to my bedroom while we wait to see whether my father will say, "What's for supper?" If he says, "What's for supper?" then it's safe for me to serve him and for Rain to sit by the table while we eat. She can stare at us and put her paws in our laps wanting food until I see my father's eyes get black and hard and that's the signal that Rain should go back to my bedroom.

If my father comes home and doesn't say anything, but walks into his own room, then Rain and I should not go near him at all. And I have to make Rain stay very quiet so she doesn't annoy him or give him a headache.

Rain knows (nose) to (two, too) stay away from my father's feet (feat) and his shoes (shoos).

3

The Rules of Homonyms

I am the only student in my classroom who's interested in homonyms. This suggests to me that most kids are not interested in homonyms. So if you want to skip this chapter, it's all right.

But if you read it, you might get interested in homonyms.*

*If you are not interested in homonyms at all, stop reading here and skip to Chapter Four.

Homonyms can be surprising and fun, and that's why I started a list of them. The list is very long. Right now it takes up four sheets of paper. The words are in alphabetical order. I try to leave space between the pairs and trios of homonyms so that I can add new ones to the list easily. But if the spaces have gotten used up and I've thought of *another* set of homonyms, then I have to rewrite the list from that point on. Sometimes this makes me cry because I have to write the words perfectly, without making any mistakes. If I make a mistake I have to start over. Josh Bartel, who is a 4'10" boy in my classroom, said to me last week, "Rose, just keep the list in your computer. Then you can add in new words wherever you want. The computer will make spaces for you. You won't have to keep rewriting the list."

But my father and I do not have a computer. Or a cell phone or a digital camera or an iPod or a DVD player. My father says those things are expensive and unnecessary. He says we can't afford them, and who needs them anyway?

So my homonyms list is on paper.

In this chapter I'm going to tell you about my rules for homonyms. But since I've realized that most kids aren't any more interested in rules than they are in homonyms, I'll tell you something fun about homonyms first. Then I'll get to the rules, and if you're still interested you can keep reading.

What's fun about homonyms is hearing a word in a sentence and suddenly realizing that it has a homonym, or maybe two (or three, but that's so rare that I don't often think about homonym quartets), and that you haven't thought of that homonym pair or trio before. For instance, yesterday, Uncle Weldon said to me, "Look how carefully Rain chews her food." And just like that I had a new pair of homonyms to add to my list.

Uncle Weldon and I were sitting at my kitchen table when he said that, and I jumped out of my chair and cried, "Oh! 'Chews' and 'choose'! That's a new homonym pair!"

Uncle Weldon gets excited about homonyms too, so he said, "Wonderful, Rose. Go find your list. Let's see if there's room for two more words."

While I was getting the list out of my backpack, I thought about the word *chew* and how it rhymes with *brew* and as I ran back to Uncle Weldon I began to shout again. "And also there's 'brews' and 'bruise'! Oh, that's a *really* good pair! Two new pairs to add to my list! This is almost a red-letter day."

So, in conclusion, that is what's fun about homonyms.*

If you've heard enough about homonyms and you don't want to learn my rules, stop reading here and skip to Chapter Four.

Now, here are my rules of homonyms. It's important

to have rules, because without them, you could get overwhelmed thinking of words that sound alike. Your list would be pages and pages and pages long. The purpose of most of my rules is to limit homonyms to words that are pure and also that are English.

ROSE HOWARD'S RULES OF HOMONYMS

1. A true pair or trio of homonyms includes no proper nouns. A proper noun names a particular person or place or thing, such as Josh Bartel or Hatford or Rice Krispies cereal. I thought about including *coax* and *Cokes* and *herald* and *Harold* on my list, but *Cokes* and *Harold* are proper nouns, not pure words. Including proper nouns would make my list too long. Luckily, *Rose* and *Rain* are proper nouns *and* regular nouns, so I was able to include them on my list.

2. A true pair or trio of homonyms includes no foreign words. I put the words *peek* and *peak* on my list, but I did not add *pique* for a trio, because *pique* is a word of French origin. Including foreign words on my list would become very difficult, because I don't know all the languages.

3. A true pair or trio of homonyms includes no contractions. *Isle* and *aisle* are on my list, but I didn't add *I'll* because it's actually a contraction of the words *I will*. Therefore it doesn't count as a pure word. (Besides, *I* is a proper noun.)

4. A true pair or trio of homonyms includes no abbreviated words. I did not add *ink* and *inc.* to my list because *inc.* is short for *incorporated*, which is clearly not a homonym for *ink*.

5. A true pair or trio of homonyms includes only words that sound *exactly* alike. Since *whine* and *wine* do not sound *exactly* alike they are not on my list. Neither are *haul* and *hall*.

I guess that's enough about homonyms for now. You probably want to get on with my story anyway, so now it's time for me to introduce the next main character to you. The next main character is my father, Wesley Howard.

Oh, one more fun thing about homonyms: The word *pair* implies *two*, but it is part of a homonym *trio*—pair, pear, and pare.

4

Some Things About My Father, Whose Name, *Wesley Howard*, Does Not Have a Homonym

Wesley Howard is my father and he's 33 years old. He was born on March 16th during a quarter moon. He's 6'1" tall. He has a scar on his cheek that is 1 ½ inches long. He got it when he was seven and his father whacked him in the face with the handle of a shovel in order to teach him not to leave his bike outside.

Some things about my father and me that are the same are that we grew up with our fathers but not our mothers, and that we live in the country.

My father's profession is mechanic at the J & R Garage.

My father has one sibling, my uncle Weldon, who is 31 years old and 6'0" tall. Uncle Weldon was born on June 23rd during the kind of moon called a full strawberry moon. My father was born at 6:39 p.m. and my uncle was born at 9:36 p.m. so their birth times are opposite when written out. Also, the numbers are all divisible by 3.

My father was 21 when I was born. He was 23 when my mother left. He was 26½ when I started kindergarten. He was 26 years and 7 months when my kindergarten teacher, Miss Croon, told him that Hatford Elementary might not be the right school for me.

"I didn't know there was another elementary school in Hatford," my father replied.

"That isn't what I meant."

What Miss Croon meant was that since I was having trouble talking to the other kindergarteners and I cried a lot and was apt to hit myself in the head with a shoe or a picture book if somebody didn't follow the rules, I might need a special school or program.

My father told Miss Croon to work harder. Teaching me was her job.

"Are you sure you don't want to look into another program for Rose?" asked Miss Croon.

"Where are the other programs?" asked my father.

"There's an excellent one in Mount Katrine."

"Mount Katrine that is twenty-two miles away?"

"Yes."

My father shook his head. "Rose will be fine right here."

In first grade, my teacher, Ms. Vinsel, called a meeting with the principal and the school psychologist and Miss Croon and my father. I don't know what happened during the meeting because I wasn't there. After the meeting my father picked me up at Uncle Weldon's office and took me home and shook me and said, "Rose, this behavior has got to stop."

And I told him that you could write out my name two ways and both ways would be pronounced the same.

For second grade I had Miss Croon again because she didn't want to teach kindergarteners anymore. Miss Croon said to my father on the afternoon of September 13th, "I believe Rose would benefit from spending part of every day in the Resource Room, Mr. Howard."

Mr. Howard, who is my father, said, "That's fine with me as long as the Resource Room isn't for retards."

For has two homonyms—four and fore.

By fourth (forth) grade Mrs. Leibler had become my aide (aid). My father said he didn't think I needed an aide, but that he wasn't going to fight Hatford Elementary. "Just stay out of trouble, Rose," he told me. And everything was fine until fifth grade when Mrs. Leibler thought up the idea of weekly (weakly) progress reports.

Now I am going to go back in time to report on my father's childhood some more. When my father was ten years old he went to school with a brown-colored two-inch-long mark on his arm and his teacher decided it was a burn. She called Child Protective Services and that very night the police arrested my father's father, and that was when my father and Uncle Weldon went into foster care.

"We were always placed together with the same family," Uncle Weldon told me once. "We weren't split up. But we never stayed with any family for very long."

My father and Uncle Weldon lived with seven foster families before my father turned eighteen.

They lived in five different towns.

They had a total of 32 foster brothers and sisters.

They went to nine different schools.

The longest they stayed with any family was 21 months.

The shortest they stayed with any family was 78 days.

One night last year when my father and I were eating supper at 6:17 p.m., I said to him, "Did you have a favorite?"

"A favorite what?" asked my father.

"A favorite foster mother."

"Yes, I did," said my father. "Her name was Hannah Pederson."

"That is very interesting," I told him, recalling Mrs. Leibler's conversational tips, "because 'Hannah' is a kind of word called a palindrome. That means you can spell it the same way whether you start at the beginning or the end. My name is not a palindrome because if you spell it backwards it's E-S-O-R, not R-O-S-E. But it does have a homonym."

My father said, "Don't get started on homonyms, Rose."

So I said, "Did you have any favorite foster brothers or sisters?"

"Yes," said my father after a moment.

"How interesting," I replied. "Did any of their names have homonyms?"

5

When We Got Rain

Now I will tell you about when we got Rain. On the Friday before Thanksgiving last year I was waiting for my father to come home from The Luck of the Irish. I knew he was at The Luck of the Irish because it was 7:49 p.m., which meant that the J & R Garage had been closed for two hours and 49 minutes. I had made hamburgers that night and I had already eaten mine because I don't like to eat dinner after 6:45 p.m. What was for dessert was Popsicles, and I had also already eaten my Popsicle, which was a Highcrest brand Orange Burst.

I was studying my list of homonyms when I saw headlights circle around the kitchen and I heard a car pull into our driveway. I decided that it was my father's car. Next I heard a door slam. Then I heard another door slam and I decided that my father had brought Sam Diamond home with him. Sam Diamond is a man who drinks at The Luck of the Irish with my father and sometimes comes here to sleep on our living room couch. After a few seconds I heard footsteps on the front porch, and then I heard a sound like a whine, which was not a sound I had ever heard Sam Diamond make.

I sat at the table and stared at the door.

My father appeared in the porch window. "Rose, for lord's sake, get up off your butt and come help me," he yelled.

I didn't want to help my father with Sam Diamond. But when I opened the front door and looked out through the screen at the rainy night I saw that my father was standing on the porch holding a thick rope in his left hand and that at the other end of the rope was a dog. The passenger in the car had been the dog, not Sam Diamond.

The rope was tied around the dog's neck. The dog was very wet.

"Where did you find a dog?" I asked my father.

"Behind The Luck of the Irish. Could you bring a towel out here so I can dry her off?"

"The dog is a she?" I asked.

"Yes. The towel?" This was my father's way of reminding me to get the towel to dry off the wet dog.

"And don't bring a white towel," my father called after me. "She's muddy."

I brought a green towel to the porch and watched through the screen door while my father wiped the dog's feet and back. "She's for you," he said to me. "You can keep her."

"She isn't wearing a collar," I replied.

"That's why she's yours. She's a stray."

"But shouldn't we look for her owners?" I asked. "They might want her back."

"If they didn't care enough to get her a collar, then they don't deserve her," said my father. "Besides, how would we find her owners? She doesn't have a collar so she doesn't have any tags."

"Is she a gift?" I wanted to know.

"What?" said my father. He stopped wiping the dog for a moment. "Yes, she's a gift, Rose. She's my gift to you."

My father had not given me many gifts.

The dog stood patiently while my father wiped her fur. She lifted her front feet one at a time when he held out the towel. Then she gazed at me and lifted her eyebrows up and down. She panted, and when she panted she stretched her lips wide so that she looked like she was smiling.

"All right," my father said to the dog. "You're dry enough to go inside." He held the door open and the dog walked into the living room, which is really just part of the kitchen, and she leaned against my legs.

I stared down at her. She stared up at me.

"You can pet her," said my father. "That's what normal people do with dogs."

So I petted her and she closed her eyes and pressed in closer.

"What are you going to name her?" asked my father.

"I will name her Rain," I replied. "You found her in the rain, and rain has two homonyms—reign and rein—so it's a special word."

"That's great, Rose. And what about 'thank you'?"

"Thank you."

That night Rain slept in bed with me. She has slept with me every night since then.

6

Who I Wait For

Uncle Weldon drives me to and from school every day. He does this because I'm no longer allowed to ride the bus, and when my father heard about that he announced that he couldn't drive me himself. He said, "Rose, what did you go and get yourself kicked off the bus for? How am I supposed to drive you to school in the morning and get to the garage at the same time? And how am I supposed to pick you up in the middle of the afternoon while I'm working?"

There are a lot of days when there's no work for my father at the J & R Garage, but on those days he likes to sleep late and then go to The Luck of the Irish.

Uncle Weldon said, "I could drive Rose to school."

Uncle Weldon works at a construction company. He has what my father calls a wuss job and what Uncle Weldon calls a desk job. He doesn't do construction. He sits at a computer. His job starts at 9:00 a.m., so he could easily drop me off at my school, which starts at 8:42 a.m. before going on to his company, which is called Gene's Construction, Inc. He said he would ask his boss if he could work through his lunch break so that he could pick me up at 2:42 p.m. and run me home every afternoon.

When Uncle Weldon mentioned that he could drive me to school, he didn't look directly at my father. He and my father and Rain and I were sitting on the front porch, and Uncle Weldon stared out at Hud Road while he spoke.

I waited for my father to say, "I can take care of this myself." But instead he lit a cigarette and stared at Hud Road too.

So then I joined them in looking at the road while I said to my father, "Did your father drive you to school?"

"He didn't have to. I didn't get kicked off the bus. Why are you asking about my father?"

I was asking because my father always says that he's not going to be the kind of father that *his* father was. He says he's going to raise me up by himself if it kills him.

This is why he doesn't accept much help from Uncle Weldon. And this was why Uncle Weldon asked his question so carefully. When my father thinks Uncle Weldon is interfering in my raising, he threatens to keep us apart, which would make my uncle and me feel very sad.

"I don't know," I said.

Rain was lying next to me on the old couch that my father had put out on the porch. She rolled over on her back and rested her head in my lap.

"You asked me a question, but you don't know why you asked it?" said my father.

"Yes."

"What about it?" Uncle Weldon wanted to know. "Could I drive her? It would solve the problem."

"It wouldn't mean you're a bad father," I said.

Uncle Weldon shifted his gaze from Hud Road to me, and his eyes opened wide. "That is certainly not what I meant."

"Well, anyway, I don't see another way around it," replied my father.

And that is how Uncle Weldon started driving me to and from Hatford Elementary. Every morning, Rain and I wait on the front porch for my uncle to come along Hud Road in his black Chevrolet Montana. When I see the truck, I kiss Rain on her head and put her inside the house. Then I climb up beside my uncle and tell him if I've thought of any new homonyms since the day before.

If I have, Uncle Weldon says, "That's great!" Then we try to think of other new homonyms that sound like the new pair, the way I did with chews/choose and brews/bruise.

After we discuss homonyms we look out the windows for a while, and then Uncle Weldon will say, "Everything all right with your father and Rain?"

The least complicated answer is yes. I don't say more unless I have to.

Sometimes Uncle Weldon will say, "Would you like to go to a movie with me this weekend, Rose?" Or maybe, "Should we take Rain on a hike on Saturday?" Then we have to think about how to ask my father for permission.

Finally we drive up in front of Hatford Elementary. Uncle Weldon and I always cross our fingers and touch our hearts before I slide out of the truck.

• • •

At the end of the day I wait for my uncle again. I stand by the front door of the school and watch the kids I used to ride the bus with as they line up for Bus #7. I step away from Monty Soderman who is missing one (won) fingernail, and who wears very heavy boots that hurt a lot when he steps on my toes (tows). I wait (weight) and hum and stand by myself and stare (stair) straight (strait) ahead so that I can see (sea) Uncle Weldon the moment he turns onto School Lane (Lain). Then I run to his truck and he smiles as he leans across the seat to open the door for me.

Sometimes we have a conversation like this:

UNCLE WELDON: How was school?

ROSE HOWARD: It was just like yesterday.

UNCLE WELDON: Exactly like yesterday?

ROSE HOWARD: No. That would be impossible.

UNCLE WELDON: Because today has a different date from yesterday.

ROSE HOWARD: And because the moon and stars are in different positions than yesterday.

UNCLE WELDON: What's the most interesting thing you learned today?

ROSE HOWARD: That if you assign numbers to the letters in "Weldon"—like 23 for W because it's the 23rd letter in the alphabet, and 5 for E, and 12 for L, and 4 for D, and 15 for O, and 14 for N—the numbers add up to 73. Guess what 73 is.

UNCLE WELDON: A prime number?

ROSE HOWARD: Yes! And that is as special as a homonym. My father's name is a prime number too. W-E-S-L-E-Y comes out to 89.

UNCLE WELDON: Really?

ROSE HOWARD: Yes, but I don't think he'll be interested.

UNCLE WELDON: Well, I'm glad your father and I have prime number names, since you and Rain have homonym names. Now nobody will feel left out.

ROSE HOWARD: I wonder if my father would let me come over to your house on Saturday. I could rewrite my homonyms list. It's getting crowded.

UNCLE WELDON: Would you like me to ask him about that?

ROSE HOWARD: Yes, but just ask if I can come over. Don't mention the list.

UNCLE WELDON: I'll do what I can.

Finger crosses, heart touches, I wave good-bye to my uncle.

7

Why I Don't Ride the Bus

I used to ride Bus #7 to school. Bus #7 made 14 stops, which was good because 14 is a multiple of 7. I was the only person at my bus stop, the second stop on the route. At the next twelve stops, every kid would walk down the aisle looking for a seat and pass by the empty space next to me. Marnie Mayhew, who lives at the prime-number homonym address of 11 Band (Banned) Lane (Lain), would flick a spitball at me as she went by. I would stare straight ahead and let it bounce off my face onto the bus floor. Then Wilson Antonelli would come along and say, "Pick it up, Retard. You're littering."

At each stop our driver, whose name was Shirley Ringwood, would look at us backward in her big glaring mirror and wait until everyone was sitting down. Then she would close the door, put Bus #7 in gear, and start driving again. And I would watch out my window to see who was following the rules of the road. There are lots of rules for drivers, and they're listed clearly in the New York State driver's manual, but many drivers don't follow them.

"Hey!" I would shout. "That man didn't use his directional before he turned the corner! Mrs. Ringwood, did you see that? He broke the law."

Sometimes Mrs. Ringwood would answer me, sometimes she just kept her eyes on the road ahead. It depended on how close to her I was sitting.

Rainy days (daze) were difficult. The rule is that if your windshield wipers are on, then your headlights must be on too. "Mrs. Ringwood! Mrs. Ringwood! I just saw three cars with their wipers on and their headlights off!" I would cry.

Marnie would start to giggle and Wilson would lean over his seat and hold out his cell phone and say, "Why don't you report that to the police, Retard?"

"They're supposed to follow the rules! They aren't following the rules!"

One day I sat down in the first row of seats so I could watch Mrs. Ringwood's driving. She slowed Bus #7 as we approached the intersection of Sandy Road and Route 9W. Then we rolled slowly by the stop sign.

"Mrs. Ringwood! You didn't come to a complete stop!" I shouted. "Mrs. Ringwood, that's against the law. It says in the manual that you *must* come to a complete stop. A *complete* stop."

Mrs. Ringwood turned onto Route 9W. "Let it go, Rose."

"Mrs. Ringwood, are your headlights on?"

A spitball hit me on the back of my neck.

"Hey, that driver wasn't wearing his seat belt. Did you see that, Mrs. Ringwood?"

We reached School Lane. Ahead was Hatford Elementary. Mrs. Ringwood turned the wheel to the right and we started to swing into our bus lane.

"Stop!" I shouted. "Mrs. Ringwood, stop right now!"

Mrs. Ringwood slammed on the brakes. "What's the matter?" she cried. She stood up to look out her window. Behind me, all the kids crowded to the other windows to see what had happened. Traffic came to a halt.

"You didn't use your directional," I said. "That's against the rules."

Mrs. Ringwood sat down again. She leaned her

forehead on the steering wheel. Then she turned around and said to me, "Are you freaking kidding?" After she parked Bus #7 she went into Hatford Elementary and spoke with the principal.

That's why I don't ride the bus anymore.

8

In My Classroom

My classroom faces southeast and has windows along one side and 21 desks for students, plus Mrs. Kushel's desk, plus Mrs. Leibler's chair, which sits next to my desk and blocks the aisle.

There are 11 girls and 10 boys in my class.

There are 2 gerbils in my class.

Our classroom rules are written on a sheet of oaktag, which is posted next to the door of our room.

Mrs. Kushel smells of apples and has a husband and a girl who is six and has the prime number name of Edie (23).

Mrs. Kushel knew last spring that she was going to get me as her student and she scheduled a conference with my father who said, "I promise Rose won't be any trouble."

When Mrs. Kushel asked what my father does about my tantrums at home, he said, "Rose doesn't have any tantrums at home, not while I'm around. She knows better." And then he said, "Ha-ha. Just kidding."

I know this because I was sitting in the waiting room outside the school psychologist's office and I could hear every word of the conference. I hear lots of things I'm not supposed to hear, and lots of things nobody else is able to hear, because my hearing is very acute, which is a part of my diagnosis of high-functioning autism. The clicks our refrigerator makes bother me, and so does the humming sound that comes from Mrs. Kushel's laptop computer. One day in school I put my hands over my ears and said, "I can't concentrate! Please turn that thing off."

"What? What thing?" asked Mrs. Leibler.

"I want Mrs. Kushel to turn off her computer," I said clearly, in the way Mrs. Leibler has taught me.

("Tell me clearly what you want, Rose," Mrs. Leibler says when I'm out of control.)

"Why do you want her to turn it off?" asked 4'10" Josh Bartel, who sits in front of me.

"Because of the humming!"

"I don't hear any humming," said Josh.

"Rose, settle down," said Mrs. Leibler.

I hear clicks and humming and whispers. And conversations in the psychologist's office when the door is almost closed.

• • •

Mrs. Kushel has been my teacher for 25 school days now.

On the afternoon of day #25 she announces to our class, "I have an assignment that will be fun for you. You're going to write a composition about a pet."

"I don't have a pet," says Flo, whose name is easy to remember because of the homonyms *flow* and *floe*.

Mrs. Kushel smiles, which is her way of saying that she doesn't mind that Flo interrupted her. "That isn't a problem," she replies, "because you may write about any pet at all. If you don't have your own pet, you may write about an imaginary one or someone else's pet."

Mrs. Kushel passes out paper and I find my pencil and stare (stair) at the door for a while.

"Rose?" says Mrs. Leibler.

"I'm thinking," I say, without looking at her.

I start writing about Rain. I try to remember what

Mrs. Kushel has said about themes, and what Mrs. Leibler has said about not working homonyms into every theme.

"Time's up," Mrs. Kushel says after 21.5 minutes. "Who would like to read aloud to the class? It doesn't matter if your composition is finished. Just read what you have so far. You can finish your work at home tonight."

Three girls and two boys raise their hands. Mrs. Kushel calls on Flo, who reads about a pet she has made up in her head, called a chickapoo, which is a cross between a chicken and a poodle. Flo says her chickapoo doesn't cluck or bark, it clarks. Everyone laughs, while I think about the clarking chickapoo just long enough to figure out that *chickapoo* is not a prime number word, but a word that is 81, which means it's divisible by 3, so it's not as good as a prime number, although it's interesting.

The next person to read is Josh Bartel, who has written about his four neon tetra fish. "My mom picked out the first fish for my sister and I last summer," he says.

I interrupt him right there. "Mrs. Kushel!" I cry. "Mrs. Kushel, Josh broke a rule. He wrote, 'for my sister and I' and that's not right."

"Rose, what have we said about interrupting?"

"But he was supposed to write, 'for my sister and me.' *Me*. 'I' isn't always correct."

"Rose, that's a comment you might make later, when Josh has finished reading," says Mrs. Kushel.

"And," Mrs. Leibler says quietly to me as Josh continues with his composition, "you might think about telling him something positive first, and then pointing out his mistake."

I put my head down on my desk.

"Rose?" Mrs. Leibler whispers.

I don't raise (rays, raze) my head. "He didn't pay attention to the rules!" I can feel tears in my eyes.

"Rose—"

"Mrs. Kushel clearly told us about that rule on September seventeenth," I say loudly into my arms.

"Do you need to step into the hall?"

I stand up suddenly and my chair shoots backward and slams into Morgan's desk.

"Hey!" she cries.

I hit the right side of my head with the heel of my hand. One, two, three, four times.

Josh is still reading about his neon tetra fish, but most of the class is looking at me now.

"Come on," says Mrs. Leibler, and she steers

42

me to the door and into the hall. "You need to settle down."

I imagine that my father will read (reed) about this in Friday's report.

9

Mrs. Leibler,
Who Sits Next to Me

Mrs. Leibler is almost always by my side. She sits next to me in Mrs. Kushel's class, and she walks with me to the girls' room and the playground. I'm the only student in fifth grade at Hatford Elementary with an aide. This leads me to believe that most fifth-graders don't need aides. Even so, twice I've heard kids in my class say to Mrs. Kushel, "It isn't fair that Rose gets so much special attention." The first person to say that was Lenora Tedesco. The second person was Josh Bartel.

Mrs. Leibler sits with me in the cafeteria too, and we eat our lunches together. I buy my lunch, the same lunch every day—an apple and a tuna sandwich and milk. Mrs. Leibler brings her lunch, which is not the same lunch every day. Sometimes she brings a sandwich, sometimes leftovers like noodles (Mrs. Leibler calls them pasta) or a chicken leg or salmon or rice and vegetables. Mrs. Leibler always says, "Would you like a taste, Rose?" and I always say no because I don't want to vary my lunch.

On Mondays Mrs. Leibler chooses two kids from our class to be my Lunchroom Buddies for the week. She keeps a list of the buddies so that everyone gets the same number of turns. Usually when she announces the buddies no one says anything.

In the cafeteria Mrs. Leibler follows me through the lunch line. When I have my apple and sandwich and milk we sit at a table, and pretty soon the Lunchroom Buddies finish getting their own lunches by themselves, and then they sit down with us.

Today is Monday and my new buddies are Flo and Anders, one name that's divisible by 3—Flo (33)—and one prime number name—Anders (61).

Mrs. Leibler nods at me. "Rose?"

I finish chewing a bite of apple and say, "I live in a house that faces northeast. Which direction do *your* houses face?"

Mrs. Leibler is raising her eyebrows at me and I remember that I'm supposed to look at Flo and Anders when I talk to them. So I lean across the table and stare into their eyes and say again, "Which direction do *your* houses face?"

Flo shrugs her shoulders and leans away from me. "Um, I don't know." She sees that Mrs. Leibler is busy opening her container of pasta, and she turns to Anders and rolls her eyes at him.

Anders rolls his eyes back at Flo and says, "I don't know either."

I think for a moment. Then I say to Anders, "You don't know which direction *your* house faces or you don't know which direction *Flo's* house faces?"

He stiffens his lips and I think maybe he's trying not to laugh. He says, "I don't know which direction anything faces."

Mrs. Leibler spills some of the pasta on her shirt, and she stands up suddenly and says, "Excuse me, I'll be right back."

"Why do you care which direction things face?" Flo asks as soon as we're alone.

Mrs. Leibler has not prepared me for this question, so I say, " 'You,' 'yew,' and 'ewe' are homonyms."

"Wow, that is *fascinating*," replies Anders.

Flo starts to giggle. "*Please* tell us more about homonyms."

I set down my apple. "I do not include abbreviated words on my list," I inform them. "Do you think 'incorporated' is actually a homonym for 'ink'?"

"Of *course* not," says Flo.

Mrs. Leibler returns to the table with a handful of napkins.

"Mrs. Leibler, Mrs. Leibler!" I say. "I'm telling Flo and Anders about the homonym abbreviation rule."

Mrs. Leibler looks at me over the top of her glasses and says, "Let's steer the conversation in a different direction. Away from homonyms. Think about some of—"

I don't want Mrs. Leibler to say anything about conversation starters in front of my Lunchroom Buddies. I feel a little bit like crying, but I don't, and I don't bang myself in the head either. Instead I say, "I have a dog named Rain." I'm about to ask, "Do *you* have any pets?" when I remember our compositions and Flo's chickapoo. "Rain eats My Pet dog food," I continue. "What does your clarking chickapoo eat, Flo?"

Flo starts to giggle again, but this time it's a true laugh. "You remembered!" she exclaims. She thinks for a moment and finally she says, "Well . . . a clarking chickapoo eats chog food."

"*Chog* food?!" exclaims Anders.

"Oh," I say. " 'Chog' for 'chicken' and 'dog.' "

Anders starts to laugh, and then Mrs. Leibler laughs too, and now instead of feeling sad, I'm happy about Mrs. Leibler and her conversation starters. Just like my father is happy that Uncle Weldon can take me to school but he was mad that Uncle Weldon thought up the solution in the first place.

10

Anders Isn't
Following the Rules

On day #32 with Mrs. Kushel, I finish two math worksheets without saying a word about the buzzing I can hear, which is Mrs. Leibler's cell phone in her purse. When I solve the last problem I turn to Mrs. Leibler and she says, "Excellent, Rose. You focused very well today."

I glance at the clock and see that there are four minutes left in math period. "May I play with the pizza game?" I ask.

Mrs. Leibler looks at the shelf where the math games are stored. "Someone else is playing with it," she says.

"It isn't on the shelf. What would you like to do instead?"

"Nothing. I'll wait for the pizza game." I always play with the pizza game if I have spare time during math, which Mrs. Leibler knows.

I wait patiently at my desk for a few moments. Then I stand up and look around the room for the game.

"There it is!" I cry. "Mrs. Leibler, it's on Anders's desk and he isn't playing with it. He's talking to Martin."

"Calm down," says Mrs. Leibler. "Why don't you ask Anders if you can have a turn now?"

"He was supposed to put it back on the shelf if he wasn't using it!" I point to Mrs. Kushel's rules, the ones posted by the door. "Look! Rule number six. 'All games, supplies, art materials, and books must be returned to their proper places when not in use.' He broke the rule!"

"I don't think he broke it on purpose," says Mrs. Leibler.

"He should have a consequence," I say.

"Mrs. Kushel will talk to him about that later."

Anders is watching me now. So is most of the class. He holds the pizza game out to me.

I don't take it. "It isn't fair," I say to Mrs. Leibler. "I was waiting for the game and now math is over."

"I'm sorry, Rose," says Anders.

I pick up my worksheets and dig my nails into them.

"Rose, please give those to me," says Mrs. Leibler.

I start to cry. "I was waiting patiently."

"I know, but don't ruin your worksheets. Give them to me and then we'll go into the hall so you can calm down."

Mrs. Leibler places the worksheets on Mrs. Kushel's desk. Then she leads me to the hallway. As we go out the door I jab my finger at the list of rules. "Number six! Number six!" I cry.

11

When Rain Went to School

On school day #33 Uncle Weldon pulls his black Chevrolet Montana into our driveway at 8:16 a.m. He sees Rain and me sitting on the porch and he waves to us by sticking his left hand out the window. Then he sticks his head out the window.

"Rose!" he calls. "Bring Rain. I don't have to go into work today. Rain can spend the day with me."

This is not part of the routine. I stand on the porch for a moment and look at Rain/Reign/Rein.

"Come on!" my uncle calls. "Rain and I will have fun together. And she won't be lonely."

"Okay." I lock the door behind me since my father has already left for the garage, and I lead Rain to the truck.

Rain sits between Uncle Weldon and me while we ride to Hatford Elementary.

"Is 'build' and 'billed' on your homonyms list?" asks Uncle Weldon as we drive past The Coffee Cup on Route 28. "I thought of that one last night."

"Yes," I say. "I really like that pair." Rain puts one of her paws in my lap and I stroke her toes. "What are you and Rain going to do today?"

"She can run around the yard while I stack firewood. Then maybe we'll go for a walk."

"Okay." Even though this is not the routine, I'm glad Rain will have a nice time with Uncle Weldon.

We reach School Lane and my uncle says, "I hope you have a good day, Rose. Rain and I will see you at 2:42." He turns into the drop-off lane and reaches across my lap to open the door.

"Bye," I say. Before I hop out, Uncle Weldon and I touch our hearts with our crossed fingers.

I run to Mrs. Leibler, who is waiting for me at the front door.

"Good morning, Rose!" she says.

We hurry along side by side through the corridors

53

to Mrs. Kushel's room. I have already hung up my sweater and am taking my homework out of my backpack when Flo says, "Hey! A dog!"

Flo is pointing to the doorway, so I turn around and look at the doorway.

There's Rain, standing under the list of class rules.

"Rain!" I exclaim. "What are you doing here?"

"Is that your dog?" asks Anders.

Rain sees me and trots across the room to my desk.

"Yes," I say.

"Is that the dog from your composition?" asks Josh Bartel.

"Yes," I say.

"What's she doing here?" Flo wants to know.

I shake my head. "I guess she followed me." Rain must have jumped out of the truck before Uncle Weldon could close the door.

"But how did she know where you were? You'd been here for, like, two minutes before she found our room," points out a girl named Parvani.

"She followed me with her nose," I tell her.

I sit on the floor and put my arms around Rain. She licks my forehead and then she sits down too.

"She's so cute!" cries Flo. She joins us on the floor. "Can I pat her?"

"Yes."

Flo runs her hand down Rain's back, and Rain makes her smiling face.

"How old is she?" asks Josh. He sits down with us, which makes three humans and one dog sitting on the floor of Mrs. Kushel's room.

"I'm not sure. My father found her one night in the rain. We don't know how old she was then."

"So she's a rescue dog?" asks Anders.

Before I can answer him, Parvani says, "How did she follow you with her nose?"

"She has a very sharp sense of smell. All dogs do. But I think Rain is special."

Everyone is crowded around us now, even Mrs. Leibler and Mrs. Kushel. Five people are patting Rain at once.

This is when I hear Uncle Weldon say, "Excuse me?" and then, "Oh, thank goodness. Rain, there you are!"

My uncle is at the door of our classroom.

"She found me," I say.

"Did she ever. She wanted to follow you after you got out of the truck. I held her back but when I finally let go of her to close the door she jumped out." Uncle Weldon turns to Mrs. Kushel. "Sorry about this," he says. "My fault. I was the one who wanted to bring Rain along this morning."

Mrs. Kushel is smiling. "No harm done."

"Rain has a smart nose," says Flo, and she strokes Rain's nose.

"You're so lucky, Rose," says Parvani.

Mrs. Kushel lets everyone visit with Rain for 3.5 more minutes before she says, "All right, class. It's time to get to work. Say good-bye to Rain."

Uncle Weldon has a leash in his pocket and he clips it to Rain's collar before he leads her out into the hall.

"Good-bye, Rain! Good-bye, Rain!" call my classmates.

In the cafeteria that day my Lunchroom Buddies and I have a lot to talk about.

12

Some More About Homonyms

Here are some more good homonyms:

grown/groan
fined/find
wrapped/rapped/rapt
patience/patients

One thing about the last pair of homonyms that is both interesting and boring is that you can use the nce/nts pattern to find other homonyms. For instance: independence/independents, presence/presents, innocence/

innocents. It's interesting because the pattern makes homonyms seem even more worthwhile, but it's boring because the pattern also makes finding new homonym pairs too easy.

But I still like all homonyms.

On school day #34 Josh Bartel says to me, "Rose, how come you go to the trouble of thinking up homonyms by yourself? You know, you can find hundreds of them by looking at Janice Joyner's List of Homonyms. All you have to do is Google 'homonyms' and you'll get to the list. It goes on forever."

I think about this. There are two problems with what Josh has said. 1. My father and I didn't have a computer before, when Josh suggested that I keep my list on a computer, and we still don't have one. 2. Another of my homonym rules is that I have to think of the homonyms myself. What is the point of looking at someone else's list and copying it? My list is original.

But what I say to Josh, as I stare into his eyes, is "I'm glad you're interested in homonyms."

13

At the End of the Day

The routine for after school is that Uncle Weldon picks me up at 2:42 p.m. and drops me off at my house between 2:58 and 3:01. Rain always greets me by jumping up and down when I open the door, licking my hands and face, and sometimes barking. Usually after that, we sit on the porch for a while. But if it's rainy or chilly, then we do not sit on the porch. At the end of school day #35 we do not sit on the porch. It's foggy and cool so we take a walk that lasts only 6.5 minutes. Rain pulls at her leash when I try to turn her around, and I know she would like a longer walk, but it's too damp and muddy for that.

"I'm going to look through the box," I say as Rain reluctantly follows me back to our yard.

On a shelf in the coat closet is a box, a hatbox. The top and bottom are held together by a white satin braid. The braid is fraying, which leads me to believe that the box and the braid are old. Also, the box used to be blue, but over the years the blue has faded to a lighter and lighter shade. Now it's pale gray.

Inside the box are things that belonged to my mother, before she left. My father doesn't care if I look through the things, so I look through them approximately every four months, which is three times a year. ($4 \times 3 = 12$)

I drag a chair to the closet, reach up high for the box, and lift it down carefully. I set it on the kitchen table. Before I open the box I study the outside of it to see if I can find any clues to my mother. But there's nothing. The box always looks the same, except that the color gets lighter and the braid gets fuzzier. I wish my mother had written something on the box, something like **These things are important to me** or **Gifts for Rose** or even just **Treasures**. But there are no words or clues of any sort. I don't even know if the box belonged to my mother or if it's just some box my father found for storing her things. My father won't talk about the box or its contents anymore.

I slide the braid aside, remove the top of the box, and look in at the familiar items. One by one, I take them out. I set them on the table in a row from left to right. I always start with the necklace that has a silver bird's nest hanging from it. Inside the nest are three pearls (purls) that are fake and are supposed to be bird's eggs. What does the necklace say about my mother? Maybe that she's a person who likes birds or birds' nests or birds' eggs.

Next I take out the seashell that looks like a tan cone and is called an auger. My mother must like augers too. She likes birds, birds' nests, birds' eggs, and augers.

The third item I take out is a photo of a black cat. Written on the back of the photo is **Midnight**. I don't remember having a cat, or any pet before my father brought Rain home. I study the cat some more. My mother likes birds, birds' nests, birds' eggs, augers, photos, and black cats named Midnight.

After the photo I examine two pins. The first is a little silver *R* for Rose. I wonder why my mother didn't take that with her. But maybe she didn't want to be reminded of me. After all, she left my father and me, so why would she want to think about us? The second pin is the kind called a hatpin. I know these things about the pins because when I was very small sometimes my father would look through the box with me and tell me about the items in it. He won't do that now, but he used to, and that is how I know that the *R* stands for Rose and that the second pin is a hatpin. It looks like a very big needle, and attached to the end, where the head of a pin should be, is a tiny clock. The clock doesn't work; the hands are just painted on. They point to 7:15. Once I asked my father if there was any reason the clock reads 7:15. He said, "No."

I wonder if my mother likes homonyms. I wonder if she likes prime numbers or rules or words.

I wonder if she left because I like those things.

The last items in the hatbox are a nickel with a buffalo on it, a tiny square of newspaper announcing that Elizabeth Parsons wed Wesley Howard in the First Presbyterian Church in Hatford, the hospital bracelet I wore when I was born, and a scarf with a picture of a rose on it.

I wish I knew (new, gnu) more about my mother. I do (dew, due) know (no) what she looks like. There are two pictures of her on the table by the couch. But I wish I knew something else besides the fact that she likes birds, birds' nests, birds' eggs, augers, photos, black cats named Midnight, pins, the letter *R*, clocks, 7:15, nickels, buffalos, her wedding announcement, my hospital bracelet, scarves, and roses.

I look at the clock on the kitchen wall. I have three

worksheets for homework tonight. It's time to start them and then start dinner. I put my mother's things back into the box in reverse order, starting with the scarf and ending with the necklace, and then I put the box back on the closet shelf.

It's later, when I'm adding Rain's My Pet dry food to her My Pet wet food, that I turn on the radio and hear the weather forecaster say, ". . . approaching storm. Hurricane Susan is expected to make landfall in three days" (daze), "and will be of epic proportions, a super-storm that could become the storm of the century."

II

The Part About
the Hurricane

14

The Storm on the Weather Channel

On the day I hear about Hurricane Susan, my father comes home from work at 5:43, which is an interesting time because the numbers are in reverse numerical order. Also, it's a good time because it means my father probably had only one drink at The Luck of the Irish after the J & R Garage closed.

For dinner I have fixed frozen chicken legs from a box, rice, and milk. Rain has already eaten her My Pet dinner. My father and I sit down facing each other at the kitchen table. Rain squeezes herself under my chair. I look directly into my father's eyes and do not say a word about homonyms.

"Why are you staring at me, Rose?" he asks.

"A superstorm named Hurricane Susan is coming," I tell him.

"Where did you hear this? From Weldon?"

"From the weather forecaster on WMHT. Eighty-eight point seven on your dial."

My father shrugs.

"It will be a storm of epic proportions," I add.

"And what are these epic proportions?"

I didn't hear the details, so I reply, "A superstorm that could become the storm of the century."

My father shrugs again. "We live inland, Rose. Well inland. A hurricane isn't going to affect us. Hurricanes stick to the coast. Sometimes they never even get to the coast. They turn around and head back out to sea."

I think for a moment. "Eighty-eight point seven on your dial is our local station."

"Yeah?"

"Our local station is talking about the superstorm."

Sometimes my father grunts. It sounds like *unh*. He grunts now. "Unh." Then he takes a swallow of milk and says, "All right. We'll look at the Weather Channel later."

As soon as we've finished dinner and I've washed the dishes, I turn on the television in the living room.

I tune it to the prime number channel of 83, the Weather Channel. Two people are sitting at a desk. Their names are written on the screen: Monica Findley and Rex Caprisi. Monica and Rex have serious looks on their faces. Behind them is a map of the United States and to the right, swirling around in the Atlantic Ocean, is a big red-colored ball that is supposed to be a picture of Hurricane Susan. It takes up a lot of the ocean.

Monica and Rex are shuffling through papers and talking to each other, and Rex turns around and points to the swirling red ball. Then a face pops up in a little box on the left-hand side of the screen and now Monica and Rex are talking to a third person whose name is Hammond Griffon. Hammond Griffon is a storm expert. A second map appears on the screen and now there's so much going on that I can't follow it all. I put my fingers over my eyes and stick my thumbs in my ears and this is when I hear, faintly, my father come into the room and say, "Rose, don't start. Just turn the TV off if it's bothering you." Then he adds, "What's the matter?"

"You turn the TV off," I tell him, without moving my hands.

I hear the TV go off. "Now *what* is the problem?"

I uncover my eyes and unplug my ears. "There was

too much on the screen." I try to think how to state my problem clearly.

My father sighs. "What?"

"Three people and two maps. And too much noise."

"I'll watch the weather later when you're asleep," my father says at last. Then he asks, "Were you scared about the storm or did you get confused?"

"I wasn't scared," I say.

He frowns at me and then he grunts. *Unh.* "Look, the storm won't get this far. The weather people just like to make a big fuss so everyone will watch their show. We might get a little wind and rain. That's all."

"Okay."

"Why don't you go to bed now?"

"Because it's too early." My routine calls for walking Rain in forty-five minutes, then changing into my pajamas, and after *that* going to bed.

"Well, don't think about the storm."

"Okay."

"I think I'll go out for a while."

"Okay."

15

Where We Live

While my father is back at The Luck of the Irish I think about the superstorm named Hurricane Susan. I wonder how many miles Hatford is from the Atlantic Ocean. I need to see a map, but I don't want to turn on the Weather Channel again. I sit on the couch in our quiet house and pat Rain for a while. Then I remember that there used to be a map of New England in our garage. I put on my sneakers and use a flashlight to shine my way across the yard to the square white garage. Rain comes along, walking so close to me that I can feel her shoulder against my leg.

I turn on the garage light and find the map. It's on my father's workbench and is not folded up properly, the creases going in the wrong directions, which makes the map puffy, not flat. I spread it out on the workbench, fold it back up the right way, then spread it out again. I put my finger on Hatford. All of the state of Massachusetts and a little of the state of New York are between my finger and the Atlantic Ocean. Maybe my father is right. Maybe we live too far inland to be bothered by a hurricane. But why was the newscaster on WMHT warning us about the superstorm?

I refold the map, making sure the creases are in the right directions, and Rain and I leave the garage and walk back to the house. I sit on the couch again. I think about Hud Road and my neighborhood.

Here are some facts about where I live:

1. The buildings on Hud Road are The Luck of the Irish, the J & R Garage, the house where I live with my father and Rain, and our garage. That is all.

2. Our house is on a little rise of land. The yard slopes from the house down to Hud Road, and Hud Road runs downhill to the J & R Garage and The Luck of the Irish at the bottom.

3. There are eight very tall trees in our yard.

Four of them are maples, two are oaks, one is an elm, and one is a birch. Behind our house are woods.

4. There are a lot of small streams in our neighborhood. They do not have names. The biggest of them runs alongside Hud, in between our yard and the road. It flows underneath the little bridge at the bottom of our driveway. I have never seen more than 10.5 inches of water there. The other little streams begin farther up Hud Road and feed into the one in front of our house, which rushes down toward the bottom.

These facts are not as interesting as homonyms or prime numbers. They are informative only. But you will need to understand them when you read later chapters, such as "Chapter 19: Rain Doesn't Come When I Call," which takes place the day after Hurricane Susan.

I finish thinking about Hud Road and our neighborhood. It's time to walk Rain. Later, when I'm in bed, listening for the sound of my father's car in the driveway, I hug Rain to me. We live inland, I say to myself. This must (mussed) be (bee) good. I say it over and over.

We live inland, we live inland, we live inland.

16

How to Get
Ready for a Hurricane

It's Monday when my father says the people on the Weather Channel just like to make a fuss so that everyone will watch their show. On Tuesday he frowns a little and says why can't the Weather Channel people be more specific about the path of the storm? On Wednesday he says *unh*, he doesn't ever remember losing power for more than four days.

Today is Thursday and my father is at home and out in our yard when Uncle Weldon drops me off after school. My father is checking to see if our gas cans are full. Rain is watching him from the couch on the porch.

Her head is resting on her front paws (pause), but her eyes are alert.

"Bye," I say to my uncle, and because I like him, I lean back into the truck before I close the door, and I look directly into his eyes. "Thank you for the ride," I say clearly.

Uncle Weldon smiles at me. "You're welcome. I'll see you tomorrow." Finger crosses, heart touches.

My uncle waves to my father through the windshield and turns the truck around.

"You're not at work," I say to my father.

"Nope, not at work. Very observant."

This might (mite) be (bee) sarcasm, which is like mockery.

Rain jumps off the porch to greet me and my father says, "I'm going into town to get supplies. Do you and Rain want to come with me?"

"Supplies for the superstorm known as Hurricane Susan?"

"Yes. Do you want to come with me?" he says again, and this is my reminder to answer his question.

"Yes, I do," I say.

I sit beside my father in the cab of our truck. Rain rides in the back. We drive down Hud Road. As we pass the J & R Garage my father waves to Jerry, who's one

of the owners. I don't know why my father isn't working today, but I don't ask him any questions.

At the bottom of Hud Road my father turns left
without using his directional.

"Hey, you didn't—" I cry.

But my father says, "Can it, Rose," without looking
at me.

We drive into Hatford and my father angles the
truck into a parking place near the hardware store.
The inside of the store is very crowded. So many people are shopping today that it's hard to walk down the
aisles.

I wring my hands. "Two, three, five, seven, eleven,
thirteen," I chant. I look at the ceiling.

"Stop it, Rose," says my father.

"Rose/rows, toad/towed, or/ore/oar."

"Rose, that's *enough*. What's the matter? Are there
too many people in here?"

"Yes."

"Do you need to go back to the truck?"

"I don't know."

"Because I could use some help." My father drags
me to a quiet corner of the store. "Everyone is out getting supplies and I'd like to get ours now before there's
nothing left. So could you just settle down and help

me?" He's taken me by the shoulders and is holding them a little too tightly. Also, his face is very, very close to mine. "Rose? Can you give me a hand here, please?"

Please/pleas.

"Okay," I say.

My father finds a cart and I focus on what we need. Paper plates and paper cups in case our dishwasher doesn't work, paper towels in case our washing machine doesn't work, water in case our water pump doesn't work, AA batteries and C batteries and D batteries for a radio and flashlights and tools.

I help my father carry our supplies to the truck. Then we drive to the grocery store and buy cereal and bread and dog food and canned soup and other things that won't go bad if our refrigerator doesn't work.

After the grocery store we drive to the Exxon station and fill up the gas cans.

• • •

That night Sam Diamond calls my father at 6:21 p.m. and they decide to go to The Luck of the Irish, so Rain and I are left alone. I realize that I could listen to the Weather Channel without looking at it. With my back to the TV I hear Rex Caprisi say that Hurricane Susan is expected to make landfall in a couple of hours and then travel up the coast.

Up the coast.

We live inland, we live inland.

I think of all the space that was between my finger and the Atlantic Ocean on the improperly folded map of New England. Even so, I turn on WMHT. The newscaster says that Hurricane Susan is an extremely large storm and will reach our area by the next night.

Isn't it funny that *right* has three homonyms and *night* only has one?

I stand in front of the cupboards where my father put away our supplies. I begin to count.

16 rolls of paper towels
24 rolls of toilet paper
2 large packages of napkins
4 packages of paper plates
2 packages of paper cups

I look at our food. I wonder if we have enough supplies for a power outage that lasts two days, four days, a week.

I wonder what will happen if a tree falls on our house.

I sit on the couch with Rain until it's time to walk her and then we go to bed and I put my arms around her and feel her chest rise and fall as she breathes.

I cross my fingers and touch them to Rain's heart.

17

Waiting

The next morning my father wakes me up by saying, "You're in luck, Rose. School is closing at noon
today."

This is an unscheduled change. It's not on our school
calendar.

I frown and sit up. "Why?"

My father is standing in the doorway, looking at Rain
and me in bed. "*Why?*" he repeats. "Because of the storm
you've been talking about all week. It's supposed to hit
sometime tonight."

"If it's going to come tonight, why are they closing
school today?"

"Geez, Rose, I don't know. So people have time to

prepare, I guess. Just go with it. You get half a day off from school, okay?"

Uncle Weldon drives me to Hatford Elementary and Mrs. Leibler walks me to my class. Everyone is talking about Hurricane Susan, the superstorm. It has made landfall south of us. Four people are dead. Thousands of others have lost their homes. Towns are flooded. Power lines are down. The storm is headed north and is expected to make an inland turn.

We live inland, we live inland.

Susan is 74, which is not a prime number name, and I haven't thought of a new homonym recently.

After Mrs. Kushel takes attendance, she asks our class if we'd like to talk about the storm.

Everyone says yes.

"This is the biggest storm in history," Josh announces. He sounds pleased.

"People have already died," says Parvani nervously.

I stand up and shout, "Two, three, five, seven, eleven, thirteen!" Before I can say, "Seventeen," Mrs. Leibler is marching me to the hall.

• • •

Uncle Weldon pulls into my driveway at 12:17 p.m. Usually he drops me off and goes right back to his job, but today he has special permission to wait with me until my father comes home. Neither of us talks about the note from Mrs. Leibler. When my father opens the envelope later he will read about the prime number incident.

At 1:21 p.m. my father returns from the J & R Garage and my uncle leaves. "We'll try to stay in touch," he says to my father and me. "Hopefully, the storm will miss us. Maybe this is a lot of hype after all."

"I'll call you tomorrow," my father replies.

Uncle Weldon heads down the driveway and I hand over the note. My father reads it as we stand on the porch. He shakes his head. "Geez, Rose, why can't you just say those numbers to yourself?"

• • •

My father stays at home the rest of the day. He stays at home after dinner too, Rain and my father and I alone in our house with the eight tall trees outside.

I can hear wind now, and a little rain.

My father turns on the Weather Channel and I sit across the room with my back to the television.

"We're right in the path," I hear my father say. "It can't miss us."

"Morgan broke a rule today," I tell him, without turning around. "She didn't raise her hand, *and* she interrupted Mrs. Kushel."

My father doesn't answer.

"You know who else broke a rule? Josh. On the very first day of school he yelled, and yelling is against the rules."

"You want to come over here and watch this like a normal person?"

"And once Anders tripped me. On purpose. And twice Flo butted into the middle of the lunch line."

"Rose, I can't hear the television."

"And also—"

My father stands up fast. He starts to throw the remote control at me, but then I think he remembers that the TV won't work without it, so he puts it down. "Go to your room," he says.

I back away from him. Rain follows me to my bed. I get out the list of homonyms. I study it and study it and then from the living room I hear the Weather Channel's Rex Caprisi say, "Check out the links posted at the bottom of the screen."

I jump off my bed. "Rain! 'Links' and 'lynx'! A new homonym!"

I run my finger down to the *L* section of the list and see that there isn't space for my new homonym pair. I'll have to rewrite the list, starting with the *L* section.

I haven't gotten any farther than lane/lain when I make an *m* instead of an *n*. I throw down my pen.

"Two, three, five!" I shout and scrunch up the paper.

My father is standing in the doorway in an instant. He looks at me and then at the paper. "I've had just about enough," he says quietly.

Rain edges herself between my father and me.

"If you can't control yourself here, at least control yourself at school. I'm sick of this. I'm sick of the notes. I'm sick of the meetings."

"But my homonyms list—"

My father stoops down and picks up the crumpled paper. "Not another word about homonyms. Put all this stuff away and go to bed. Right now."

My father doesn't leave the doorway, so Rain and I have to change our schedule for the second time that day. I slide under the covers with my clothes on. Rain lies warily next to me.

We both have to pee.

18

Storm Sounds

My father closes the door to my room, so Rain and I lie in the darkness. I can see a strip of light under my door and hear the sounds of the Weather Channel.

I can't fall asleep, even with my hand resting on Rain's sleek back.

The wind grows louder and louder. It's as loud as a train. Rain whimpers.

The television sounds disappear and then the strip of light dims, which is how I know my father has gone to bed.

The rain falls harder until it's thundering on our roof. Beside me, Rain begins to shake.

In (inn) the yard the trees creak (creek) and crack. Branches snap off.

Something heavy blows against my window. It makes a bang and I grab Rain, but the window doesn't break (brake).

I get out of bed and tiptoe to the door. I open it and listen. Nothing but (butt) storm sounds. I peer (pier) around the corner at my father's door. It's closed. No light shines underneath.

I go back to bed, leaving my door open.

My clock says 11:34 p.m. when I hear (here) a tree crash down in our front yard.

It says 1:53 a.m. when a violent gust of wind hurls something against our (hour) front door, and I wonder what we left outside. Rain shakes until the bed vibrates.

The clock says 3:10 a.m. when I hear a ferocious crack from somewhere, maybe the street, and then my clock blinks off and all the humming sounds in the house come to a stop.

Our power has gone out.

I hug Rain as tightly as possible and finally I fall asleep.

When I awaken there's dim light seeping around my window shades. The house is quiet. The storm must be nearly over.

Rain is not in my room.

19

Rain Doesn't Come When I Call

On our kitchen counter is a clock that is not electric. It's round and blue, and on the face is a drawing of an ocean wave. Above the wave are the words *Atlantic City*. The morning after the storm, I tiptoe out of my bedroom and into the very quiet kitchen. The first thing I look at is the clock. The hands are pointing to 8:05. Next I turn around to see if my father's door is open. It is not. I pick up our phone and listen for a dial tone. Nothing. I press a few buttons. Still nothing. We have no electricity and no telephone.

I walk to the window in the living room and look

outside. The day is very dark and wet. Rain is still falling, but gently, as if it might stop soon. The leaves on the trees are fluttering a little, but the wind is not roaring like it was during the night.

In our yard two trees have fallen, the birch and the elm. The birch tree came up by its roots. The tips of its branches are resting on the porch roof. The elm tree snapped just above the ground. It fell in the other direction, across the road, and took the power lines with it. Also, one of our oak trees split down the middle, and the top part snapped off another. There are branches and leaves everywhere I look.

I peer sideways over to the driveway, which is covered with branches and leaves like everything else, and follow it to the road.

I draw my breath in tight. I realize that I can see the stream that runs alongside Hud. This is the first time I've been able to see the water from so far away. As I mentioned in "Chapter 15: Where We Live," there has never been more than 10.5 inches of water in the stream. But now the water is so deep that it's flowed over its banks and flooded both the road and the lower part of our yard. It's rushing along fast and hard and swollen like a river, and it couldn't fit under our bridge, so it roared over it. The bottom of our drive has washed away. Sturdy pieces of lumber are breaking apart and hurtling down Hud.

  We are stuck on our property. Even after the water recedes, the stream will still be there, with no driveway bridging it. I turn around, wondering whether it's okay to wake my father. I want to ask him about the bridge and hear (here) his thoughts on being stranded.

  I'm about to knock on his door when I realize that I haven't seen (scene) Rain. She's not in the kitchen or the living room. I go back to my room and look under my bed. Sometimes Rain hides there if she gets scared.

  No Rain.

  I check the bathroom.

  No Rain.

  I look in the kitchen and living room once more.

  "Rain?" I call. "Rain?"

  Nothing.

  I call louder. "*Rain?*"

  Suddenly the door to my father's room bursts open. "Rose, quit yelling. I let Rain outside. She had to pee."

  "You let her outside? When?"

  "I don't know. A while ago."

  "Did you let her back in?"

  "No."

  "Why didn't you?"

"Because it was *early*. I went back to sleep. She's probably on the porch."

I forget about the trees and the water and the driveway and being stranded. I fling open the front door.

The porch is wet. Everything is dripping, and the couch is soaked.

Rain is not there. I call her name again. Then I step onto the porch in my bare feet. I stand at the top of the steps and call, "Rain! Rain! Rain! Rain!" into the gray morning.

The only sound I hear is dripping.

I begin to breathe very fast.

I think this is a sign of panic.

"Two, three, five, seven, eleven," I say. "Two, three, five, seven, eleven."

20

Why I Get Mad at My Father

I sit in a chair at the kitchen table.

Something has happened to Rain.

My father let her outside and she didn't come back.

This is not like her.

She may be lost.

I stand at the window again and gaze out at the rushing water, at the fallen trees, at the bottom of our yard that now looks like a pond.

"Find her?"

I jump. I turn around to see my father. He's standing in the doorway to his bedroom wearing an undershirt and boxer shorts.

"What time did you let her out?" I ask.

"Does that mean you didn't find her?"

"She doesn't come when I call."

"Why can't you just answer me? Say, 'No, I didn't find her.'"

"No, I didn't find her. What time did you let her out?"

My father scratches his neck and sits at the kitchen table. "Power's out," he says. "Phone too?"

"I have to answer your questions, but you don't have to answer mine?"

I see a mean little smile on my father's mouth, but all he says is, "Seven fifteen."

Seven and one and five add up to thirteen, which is a prime number, but in this case I don't think it's a good thing. "She's been gone for over an hour," I reply.

"Now you answer my question. Is the phone out too?"

"Yes. Why didn't you watch Rain when she went outside?"

"Rose."

"But why didn't you?"

"Rose, you're driving me crazy."

"Well, why didn't you wake me up?"

"What? When Rain went out? I don't know. Because we always let her out by herself and she always comes back to the porch."

"She hasn't been out during a storm before."

"Did you eat breakfast yet?"

"I was looking for Rain."

"Did. You. Eat. Breakfast. Yet."

"No."

My father starts pulling out supplies. He sets paper bowls and paper cups on the table, a box of cereal, and milk from the fridge, which is dark inside. "The milk is still okay," he says, sniffing it.

I walk from the window to the table and back to the window. I open the front door. I call, "Rain! *Rain!*"

"Breakfast is ready," says my father.

"Rain is missing." I step back inside.

My father goes to the window. "What a mess," he says.

"The bridge over the driveway washed away," I tell him. "We're stuck here."

"Damn."

"I wish we could call Uncle Weldon."

"What's he going to do?"

"Help me look for Rain. Why didn't you watch her when she went out?"

"I've already answered that question, Rose. Now let's eat."

I stand at the window. I pace into my bedroom and

back to the kitchen. "Why didn't you check to see if she came back?"

My father slams his hand on the table and the carton of milk jumps. He looks at the Atlantic City clock. "It's 8:30," he says, "and already I've had it with you."

Eight thirty is when my father has had it with me, and also when I notice that Rain's collar is hanging on the doorknob. That's where I left it last night, before my father made Rain and me go to bed without peeing.

Rain is lost outside and she isn't wearing her collar.

She has no identification.

My father is the one who let her out. That's why I'm mad at him.

21
Rain's Nose

All dogs have smart noses, but Rain's must be especially smart. I think of the day she followed me through the hallways at school until she found me in Mrs. Kushel's room. Her nose had to sort through the smells of dozens of kids and teachers, and choose just mine to track.

I remember Parvani saying, "You're so lucky, Rose." She meant lucky to have Rain, a dog with such a smart nose.

I can't eat the cereal my father fixes for me. I leave the table and stand at the front door again.

"A watched pot never boils," says my father. He slurps some cereal and washes it down with warm Coke from a can.

"What?" I say.

"Never heard that expression? It means . . ." My father pauses. "It means, well, it means don't keep standing there. Rain will come back when she's ready."

I turn around to face my father. "Rain has a smart nose," I tell him.

"Unh."

"She does. Even if she got turned around in the storm her nose will help her find her way home."

"Okay then. Come eat your breakfast."

• • •

The day is long and dark. The rain stops falling and the wind stops blowing, but the sun doesn't come out. Our house is cold. My father puts on pants and a flannel shirt. He makes a fire in the woodstove. I think I would feel warmer if Rain were here.

After breakfast I ask if I can go outside and search for Rain.

My father stands on the front porch and considers this. At last he says, "You can go outside, but don't leave our yard. There are power lines down and you could electrocute yourself. Don't go near any wires, and don't go near any water either. You have no idea how powerful rushing water is."

"Could Rain swim in it?" I ask.

"In rushing water? Probably not."

I walk all around our yard. I call, "Rain! Rain! Rain!" I have to step over branches and climb over the fallen trees.

No sign of Rain.

I walk down the slope toward Hud Road, but stop when I reach the water. The water in our yard is not moving fast, but I don't know how deep it is. The water by the road is moving fast. It's rushing, just like my father said. I throw a branch in and it disappears immediately. I don't see it again.

I call for Rain, but the water is so loud I can barely hear my voice.

I go back inside. My father is sitting at the kitchen table trying to tune the battery-powered radio.

"Piece of junk," he mutters, just before a voice comes booming into the room.

"It works," I say, and then remember my father's sarcasm remark about being observant. I wait for him to say something, but he just keeps fiddling with the knobs.

Finally he tunes into a weather alert about a flood warning.

"What a surprise," says my father. "A flood warning."

This sarcasm is directed at the radio.

For lunch we each eat a banana and an untoasted bagel with peanut butter. Then my father says, "Might as well begin cleaning up the yard. There's nothing else to do."

"I wish we could talk to Uncle Weldon," I say.

"Well, we can't. The phone doesn't work and the roads aren't passable."

• • •

We work in the yard all afternoon. By the time the light fades, most of the branches have been piled up to use for kindling when they dry out. The trees will be cut up later with power saws.

My father starts to walk toward our dark house. I stand in the yard for a moment and look all around. Maybe I will see Rain's eyes shining in the last of the daylight. I stare and stare (stair and stair).

Nothing.

• • •

I have trouble sleeping that night. I lie in bed and think about Rain. I get up five times and check the front porch to see if she's followed her nose home. But I don't see her.

Finally I fall asleep. I don't wake up until morning, when my father knocks on my door. He steps inside and says, "School is going to be closed indefinitely." He's carrying the battery-powered radio.

"Is Rain on the porch?" I ask.

My father sighs. "No."

"What are we going to do today?"

He gestures out the window. "Sun is shining. It's a little warmer. We can work in the yard again."

"Okay. How long do you think indefinitely is?"

My father shakes his head. "Rose, indefinitely is indefinitely. It means they don't know."

So indefinitely implies uncertainty. I don't like uncertainty.

"Couldn't someone make a guess?" I ask. "I really need to know."

"Sorry. You're going to have to wait." My father holds out the radio. "I've been listening to the news," he says. "The power is out everywhere. Millions of people are in the dark. *Millions*. It could take weeks to restore it. And your school won't open until the power is back."

But I need my routine.

Most of all I need Rain.

• • •

My father and I eat dry cereal and crackers with peanut butter for breakfast. Then we step into our yard again. My father looks at the fallen trees. I walk toward Hud and look at the water. It seems a little lower in our yard. But all around me I can still hear a loud whooshing sound. Whooshing and roaring. The little brooks have become streams and the streams have become rivers. I can imagine that if they washed away our bridge, they washed away other things. Bigger things and smaller things. Houses maybe, and all kinds of living creatures.

I look at the power lines that still lie across Hud. I look in the direction of The Luck of the Irish and see the trees that have fallen across the road, blocking the way. I realize it will be a long time before Uncle Weldon can visit us.

Late in the afternoon, when my father is getting tired of buzzing through trees with his chainsaw, I see someone making his way along the road.

"John!" my father calls.

The man waves to him. Then he wades to the side of the road and stands near the spot where our bridge should be. "Guess you're stranded," says John, who has a prime number name (47) and who may be someone my father knows from The Luck of the Irish.

My father puts one hand on his hip. He wipes his

brow on his sleeve. "Yup. It'll be a while before this is fixed. Maybe I can build a temporary bridge over the stream. Hear any news?"

"The flooding around here is terrible," says John 47. "Whole towns washed away. Not ours, but others. People's houses gone. Plenty of others will have to be condemned. Don't know where the owners will go."

My father shakes his head. "What a mess."

• • •

By the time my father and I go to bed I realize that Rain has been missing for 37 hours, another number that is prime but not good.

I lie in my bed wearing layers of clothes because the house is so cold. I listen to the rushing water outside.

For the first time I think that maybe Rain has gotten so lost that she won't be able to find her way home after all.

22

What Must
Have Happened

I lie (lye) awake in (inn) my bed for (fore, four) a long time (thyme). I can't fall asleep. Even though my room is chilly I crack the window open. I listen to the rushing water. I imagine tiny trickles of water on hilltops, dripping down to join brooks and streams, gathering force and speed, and meeting (meting) with rivers. Then I imagine all those trickles and brooks and streams and rivers swollen with the 15 inches of rain that fell during Hurricane Susan. That's how much rain we got in 12 hours. Fifteen inches. More than a foot. My father heard it on the battery-operated radio.

I try to picture what our driveway looked like as the bridge suddenly loosened, how the boards must have cracked and shifted before starting to break away and float off down Hud. I remember what my father said about the force of moving water, and what John 47 said about houses washing away.

Finally I think I know what happened to Rain. This is my idea: After my father let Rain out in the storm she walked across our yard in the dim light. She's very smart and she has a very smart nose, but she didn't know enough to stay away from the water at the bottom of our yard. It was new to her. Rain is curious, and maybe she leaned over to see what her nose could tell her about the rushing water. Maybe she saw something floating in it and stepped closer for a better look. Or maybe she just wanted a drink.

Whatever happened, Rain got too close and the water swept her away. She's a good swimmer, but she might have been swept very far downstream before she managed to climb out. When she finally reached a place where she could get out of the water she sniffed and sniffed, but nothing smelled familiar to her. She couldn't find my trail because she was too far from me. There was wind, there was floodwater, and there were unfamiliar smells. Rain got confused. She got turned around. She didn't know which way to go, and she started walking in the wrong direction.

In conclusion, I think Rain was washed a very long distance from our house. And because of that it will take her a very long time to find her way back to me.

Where are you, Rain?

My heart starts to pound.

Two, three, five, seven, eleven, thirteen.

III

The Next Part

23

Why My Father Gets Mad at Me

The next day, which is Monday, is sunny with a blue sky, and at 8:00 a.m., the moderate prime number temperature of 59 degrees. When I stand on our porch with my back to the yard, I would not think that there had been a superstorm just 60 hours before. But when I turn around I see the fallen trees and our soggy lawn and the stream that runs straight down Hud, with no bridge over it at the bottom of our drive. I remember that my father and I are still stranded.

Also, Rain is still missing.

Also, the power is still out and so is our phone. The

refrigerator has warmed up, and last night my father threw out everything that was in it and everything that was in the freezer. We have no ice left and only a few more bucketfuls of water for flushing the toilet.

"What do we do when we can't flush the toilet anymore?" I ask.

My father is sitting at the kitchen table eating a breakfast of tuna, which he's scooping straight out of the can, an apple, and a bottle of ginger ale. He doesn't mind warm soda. "We go in the woods," he replies.

I study his face. I look for humor clues, such as a smile. I don't think he's being funny, so I say, "How do we go in the woods?"

"What kind of question is that? You just stand behind a tree and pee."

"I don't want to pee in the woods." It doesn't seem sanitary.

"Unh."

"What are our other options?"

"What do you mean?"

"What else could we do besides pee behind a tree?"

"I don't know. Pee in a bucket."

That sounds a little better. "Could I put the bucket in the bathroom?"

My father shrugs. "Knock yourself out."

"What?"

Now my father sighs, which is probably an indication of annoyance. "It means do whatever you want, okay? If it makes you happy to pee in a bucket in the bathroom, then pee in a bucket in the bathroom. But you'll have to clean the bucket out. I'm not going to do it for you."

I pour cereal into a bowl, sit down across from my father, and eat the cereal dry. "What are we going to do today?" I want to know.

"Keep sawing up the trees."

"I wish we could visit Uncle Weldon."

My father gestures out the window. "Has a bridge magically appeared at the bottom of the driveway?"

I turn and look. "No."

"Then we can't visit Weldon. Period. End of discussion."

• • •

After breakfast my father refills the gas tank in the chainsaw. He gets back to work buzzing through the trunks of the fallen trees. I am not allowed within 10 feet (feat) of the chainsaw, which is good because it makes a very loud noise. My job is to stack the smaller logs on the woodpile. When I can't stand the noise I take a break, put my hands over my ears, and wander around our yard. I stand by the road and look at the water, which isn't gushing so fast anymore. I wonder how far Rain could have been carried by the water on Saturday. I wonder how far she might have walked in the wrong direction after she got out of the water.

I wait until I hear the chainsaw stop for a moment and then I call to my father, "Why didn't you wake me up when you let Rain outside during the storm?"

"For Pete's sake, Rose, haven't we been over that already?"

"But why didn't you?"

"I will answer that question one more time and then I don't want to hear about it again. I didn't wake you up because Rain has been outside plenty of times by herself and she always comes back. I didn't think it was necessary. Besides, the storm was almost over."

"Why didn't you put her collar on before she went out?"

"Rose! Enough!"

"But this is a new question. This is the first time I've asked you about her collar."

My father pulls the cord on the chainsaw. Nothing happens.

"She isn't wearing her collar so she doesn't have any identification," I tell him.

"I understand that."

"So why did you leave her collar on the door?"

My father turns away from me, shaking his head. He stomps his foot on the ground, and then he pulls the cord violently. The chainsaw lets out a roar that might be as loud as a jet plane, and I cover my ears. With my hands still over my ears I walk in a circle around my father, keeping 10 feet between us, until I'm facing him. "Why didn't you put her collar on?" I yell.

My father's face is hard. He turns off the chainsaw and drops it on the ground. He walks toward me very slowly and something inside me says to run. So I do. I run into the house and slam the door behind me. When I look out the window my father is walking back to the chainsaw. I wait until I hear its roar and then go to my room and lie on my bed.

Sometimes when I'm upset Rain finds me and lies down beside me. She rests her head on my shoulder and looks into my eyes, and I can feel her breath on my cheek.

But Rain is not here now because my father didn't put her collar on when he let her outside during a superstorm.

24

I Telephone
Uncle Weldon

Something good happens the next day. I walk into our kitchen early in the morning and the first thing I notice is that the refrigerator is humming. The second thing I notice is that the kitchen feels warmer. The third thing I notice is that the little table lamp in the living room that my father sometimes leaves on overnight is shining.

The power is back on. It didn't take weeks after all.

I pick up the telephone and hear a dial tone.

The phone is back on too.

I almost knock on my father's door to tell him the

news, but then I look at the Atlantic City clock and see that it's only 6:20, too early to wake him.

It isn't too early to call my uncle, though.

When he answers he sounds sleepy, but not mad.

"Uncle Weldon!" I shout. "It's me, Rose! Everything is working again."

"Rose!" Uncle Weldon sounds as excited as I am. "Are you all right?"

"Yes," I say, since I am not injured.

"I kept trying to drive to your house but too many trees are down. I couldn't get through town. Even last night."

"Our bridge washed out," I say, "so we can't leave our yard. Uncle Weldon?"

"Yes?"

"Rain is gone."

"What?"

"Rain is gone." I tell him how my father let my dog out on Saturday morning during a superstorm without her collar.

"Oh, Rose," says my uncle. "That's awful."

"I don't know what to do. We can't look for her because we're stuck here. And I couldn't call the police because our phone didn't work."

"The police?"

"So they could search for her," I say.

There is a short silence at my uncle's end of the phone, and then he says, "The police have a lot to do right now anyway. The roads have to be cleared, and some people are still stranded in their houses, surrounded by water. We'll have to look for Rain by ourselves." He pauses. "Are you sure you're all right?"

"We're a little tired of peanut butter and tuna fish," I say. "And I had to pee in a bucket because we ran out of water. And also some trees fell down but none of them landed on the house."

"How are you doing without Rain?"

I'm not sure how to answer that.

"Rose?"

"Well, without Rain I don't have to fix her meals, and I don't have to walk her."

"But how do you feel?"

"I feel that I would like to find her."

"It sounds like you're a little lonely," says my uncle.

Now I understand. "Yes, and worried. And sad. Uncle Weldon, how do you look for a lost dog?"

"I guess we'll start by putting an ad in the paper. We can put up Lost Dog posters too. But those things may have to wait a few days, although it's a good sign that the power's on."

Since the power was back, my father and I watched

television that morning. We tuned into the news. We found out that most of the roads in Hatford were expected to be cleared by the end of the day. We found out that school might open next Monday.

"Now that Weldon can drive through town," my father said, "maybe he can buy some supplies and we can start building a temporary bridge over the stream."

"Maybe he can go to the grocery store," I added.

"Maybe. Our grocery store is under six feet of mud. So's the hardware store. He'll have to drive all the way to Newmark to go shopping."

• • •

That night we eat supper in front of the television. I hear a newscaster who's giving a crime report say, "A complicated crime began simply, under the guise of friendship."

I turn to my father. "Guise?" I say. This is exciting. "Guise? How do you spell 'guise'?"

"How should I know?"

I look it up in our old dictionary. It takes a while to find it. Then I run to my room and turn to the *G* section of my homonyms list. I add: guise/guys.

Suddenly I feel more hopeful about Rain. I open my school notebook and at the top of a blank page I write: How to Look for a Lost Dog.

25

How to Look
for a Lost Dog

K *nock, knock, knock.*

The next morning I'm awakened by the sound of knocking on our front door. Now that the power is on, I don't have to go into the kitchen and look at the Atlantic City clock to see what time it is. I can sit up in bed and look at my clock radio. Seven forty-one. Who is knocking on our door at this early non-prime-number time?

Maybe it's someone who has found Rain! But then I remember that she wasn't wearing her collar because of my father, so how would anyone know where she lives?

There is one other logical answer to the question, which is that our visitor is Uncle Weldon.

I run into the living room and peer onto the porch.

My uncle is standing there with a bag, which is probably full of groceries.

I fling open the door.

"Rose!" Uncle Weldon cries. He sets down the bag and swoops me into his arms, which I don't mind (mined) as much as I thought I might (mite).

"Hi, Uncle Weldon," I say when I'm on my feet again. "How did you get here?"

"I had to park at the bottom of the road, cross the stream where it's narrower, and walk up the hill to your house."

"Thank you for coming. I have a plan."

"You do? What kind of plan?"

"A plan for finding Rain. I'm going to get to work on it right now."

"Don't you want to see what I brought?"

"Yes." I peek into the bag. Fruit. Milk. Butter. Lettuce. Carrots.

"Did you go to the grocery store in Newmark?" I ask. Then I remember to say thank you again.

"You're welcome." Uncle Weldon smiles at me. "Yes, I went to Newmark yesterday. It was quite a drive. You

117

wouldn't believe all the homes that were destroyed. Completely destroyed."

My mind is mostly on dog-finding plans, but something occurs to me. "Where are the people?"

"The people whose homes were destroyed?"

"Yes. Are they dead?"

"Heavens, no," says Uncle Weldon. "They're living in shelters. Hatford High has been turned into a shelter. You might be going back to school on Monday, but the high school kids won't be going back any time soon."

"I'm glad the people aren't dead," I say. "Do you want me to wake up my father?"

Uncle Weldon shakes his head. "Let him sleep. I'll put the groceries away, you and I can have breakfast, and then I'll go get the truck. Your father can help me unload the building supplies from it. We're going to start work on the temporary bridge today."

Uncle Weldon and I eat breakfast together at the kitchen table. When we're finished, we cross our fingers and touch our hearts with them. Then I go to my room and spread a map out on my bed. It's the map of New England from our garage. I feel happy because it was folded properly and all the creases were going in the right directions. Next I open a phone book. It's our county phone book. Last night I looked through the business pages and found the section listing animal shelters. There were more than I had expected.

I have everything I need: the map, the phone book, the phone, a little pad of paper, and a pen.

It's time to put my plan into action.

HOW TO LOOK FOR A LOST DOG,
BY ROSE HOWARD

1. Circle your hometown on a map.

2. Circle the towns where dog shelters are located. (Consult the phone book.)

3. Next to each town, write down the names of the shelters located there.

4. Find a compass, place the point on your hometown, and draw a circle all around your town. This circle should be about 15 miles from your town.

5. Draw a bigger circle that's about 30 miles from your town.

6. Draw a bigger circle that's about 45 miles from your town.

7. Draw a bigger circle that's about 60 miles from your town.

8. Make a list of the shelters in each circle, one list per circle.

9. Phone the shelters, starting with the list of shelters that are closest to your town.

10. Keep phoning until you find your dog.

I take the map and my lists into the kitchen. My father is awake now, finishing his breakfast and talking to Uncle Weldon. I hold up the map.

"What's that?" asks my father.

"It's my plan for finding Rain." I show him and Weldon the circles and my lists. "I'll start calling the shelters in the smallest circle and work my way out," I say.

"Very organized," says Uncle Weldon. "A very smart plan."

"Plus it will keep you busy," says my father.

There's a chance that my father wants me busy so

that I won't ask him any more questions about letting Rain outside without her collar.

"I have a new homonym," I announce. "'Guise' and 'guys.'"

Then I take the map and the lists into my room and close the door.

26

Someone Calls
Me Ma'am

The first shelter on my list is called Creatures of Comfort. I'm not sure what that means, but it doesn't matter. Creatures of Comfort is located just seven miles away, outside the village of Effingham. I dial the number.

"Hello," says a voice.

"Hello," I say. "My name—"

But the voice continues talking. It sounds like it belongs to a robot. "Due to flooding, all services at Creatures of Comfort have been suspended. Sheltered animals are temporarily being housed at the Holiday

Inn in Bellville. Please call back at a later time, or visit the Holiday Inn. We apologize for the inconvenience."

The voice stops talking.

I look down at my list. I had planned to cross out each shelter after I called it, but now I can't cross out Creatures of Comfort because I haven't actually spoken to anyone there. I'll have to call back another day. I realize I'm going to need a code in order to keep track of my calls. I think for a moment. Then I write today's date by Creatures of Comfort, and next to that: CB. CB means Call Back.

I dial the number of the second shelter on the list, Rescue Me.

"Hello," says a voice and I wait for the rest of the message. "Hello?" the voice says again.

The voice must belong to a real person.

"Hello," I say. "My name is Rose Howard, and I'm looking for my dog. She got lost during the storm."

"Hi, Rose." The voice sounds kind. I think it's a woman's voice. "I'm sorry about your dog. What does she look like?"

I describe Rain, and add that my father let her out in a superstorm without her collar. "Oh, dear," says the woman. "Well, we don't have any dogs here that match Rain's description. But dogs and cats that were separated from their owners are turning up every day. I'll take down your information so we can call you if anyone brings in a small blond dog with white toes."

"Seven white toes," I remind her.

"Yes, seven white toes. That's a good identifier."

I give the woman my name and phone number and tell her I'll check back in a few days. I look at my list again. Next to Rescue Me I write: CBIAFD. This means Check Back In A Few Days.

I call Furry Friends, the third shelter on the list. A man answers and I tell him about Rain.

"Well, ma'am," he says, "we're a very small shelter, and only two dogs have been brought in since the storm—a poodle and a Yorkshire terrier. I'm sorry."

I give the man my name and phone number, hang up, and write: CBIAFD. There are still seven shelters to call before I can go on to the second list. When I have called all seven I look at the column I've made on the left-hand side of the paper. It reads: CB, CBIAFD, CBIAFD, CBIAFD, CB, NOATP (that means No One Answered The Phone), CB, CBIAFD, MPWWTTAK (Mean Person Who Wouldn't Talk To A Kid), CB.

So far there is no sign of Rain.

• • •

I spend the rest of the morning calling shelters. My father and Uncle Weldon work on the temporary bridge. At lunchtime we sit in the kitchen and eat nice, fresh, cold food from the refrigerator. Then I go back to my lists and my father and uncle go back to the bridge.

By the end of the afternoon I have called every shelter on all of my lists and I have even called several of them a second time. (I decide to ask Uncle Weldon to call the mean person.) No one has seen Rain, but she could still be wandering. I will have to do a lot of phoning before school starts again.

• • •

Uncle Weldon stays for supper.

"What about the ad?" I say when my father has served us hot dogs.

"What ad?" asks my father.

Uncle Weldon clears his throat. "I told Rose I'd put an ad in the paper about Rain."

"Unh."

"Don't you miss her?" I ask my father.

"Rain? Of course I miss her."

"Then why did you let her out—" I start to say.

My father jerks his head up so fast that I jump backward in my chair.

Uncle Weldon frowns. "What's wrong?"

"If she asks me that *one more time*," says my father, "I swear I'll—" My father stops talking suddenly. He's looking at his brother, and so am I. I see something in Uncle Weldon's eyes that hasn't been there before.

"Enough," Uncle Weldon says quietly to my father. "Enough."

I leap out of my chair and dance around the table. "Two, three, five, seven!" I cry.

"Settle down, Rose. Settle down." Uncle Weldon pats my chair. "Come back and finish your supper."

" 'Settle down, Rose. Settle down. Come back and finish your supper,' " I repeat. "Uncle Weldon, you didn't say any homonyms except my name."

My father is holding his hot dog in midair and glaring at my uncle and me.

"That's all right, Rose," says Uncle Weldon, "because guess what. I thought of a new homonym for you today. How's this? 'Packed' and 'pact'?"

I forget about my father. "That's a perfect one!" I exclaim. "It fits all the rules." I think for a moment. "And if you follow that pattern, how about 'tacked' and 'tact'?"

"Brilliant." Uncle Weldon grins at me. "After supper we'll work on your list."

"Okay." I glance warily at my father. I feel like Rain, trying to figure out what kind of mood he's in.

"Did you know," I say as we're finishing our supper, "that if you add up the numbers of our names and subtract the numbers of Rain's name you come out with a hundred and seventy-seven, which is *not* a prime number?"

Uncle Weldon frowns, thinking this over. "Is that good or bad?" he asks finally.

Before I can answer, my father says, "Who the hell cares?"

27

My Story Is Such a Sad One

On Monday, 10 days after Hurricane Susan, my school re-opens. Halloween has come and gone, but I don't think anyone noticed. Uncle Weldon arrives at my house at the usual time. I am waiting for him on the front porch, only now I am alone. This is because my father let Rain outside without her collar during a superstorm.

The air is cool and the morning is sunny. As soon as I see my uncle's truck I run across our yard to the temporary bridge and walk very carefully along the planks. I don't want to fall into the stream below, even though now there isn't much water down there. Parked in the road in front of our house is an old yellow car my father borrowed from Sam Diamond. He has to leave it in the street since we can't drive over our temporary plank bridge. But at least we aren't stuck on our property anymore.

I climb into Uncle Weldon's truck, and as soon as I've closed the door, I announce, " 'Praise,' 'prays,' and 'preys.' "

Uncle Weldon smiles at me. "Excellent. Was there room for that on your list?"

"Yes," I say. "There was room."

"Any word from any of the shelters?"

I shake my head. "No. No word."

"Are you nervous about going back to school?"

I think for a moment. "Yes. I am nervous." My father drove me by my school yesterday so I could see it, and it looked fine, but I'm still nervous.

"What are you nervous about?"

I shake my head.

I don't know.

• • •

Mrs. Leibler walks me to Mrs. Kushel's room and I see my desk. It looks like it did before Hurricane Susan. So does the rest of the room. Mrs. Leibler sits in her chair. I sit in mine. I begin to feel calmer.

The bell rings and Mrs. Kushel stands at the front of the room and smiles at us. "Hello, class," she says. "I'm glad to see you here. And I'm glad to be here with you. The last week or so has been pretty scary. But now it's time to get back to work. Before we do that, though, I think some of you might want to talk about your experiences during the storm."

I can't help myself. I leap out of my chair and say, "We can't start yet, Mrs. Kushel! Anders and Lenora aren't here."

Mrs. Leibler pulls me back into my seat and gives me a look that is most likely a warning look.

"I was just getting to that, Rose," says Mrs. Kushel. "I'm sorry to say that Anders and Lenora won't be in our class any longer. Their families had to move."

Flo raises her hand and says, "Their houses washed away."

"Are they okay?" asks Parvani. Her voice shakes a little. "I mean, are Anders and Lenora okay?"

"They're fine," Mrs. Kushel replies. "Promise. Their families have left to live with relatives."

"Could we write to them?" asks Parvani.

"That's a wonderful idea," says Mrs. Kushel. "We'll

write letters to Anders and Lenora this afternoon. Now, who would like to talk about their experiences?"

One by one my classmates talk about the last week and a half.

"My sister broke her arm," says Morgan. "She fell down our stairs when the lights were out."

"I wanted to go trick-or-treating," says Martin, "but my parents said Halloween was cancelled."

"We have to live on the second floor of our house until all the mud gets cleaned out of the first floor," says Flo. "Our house stinks."

Mrs. Kushel turns to me. "Rose, would you like to tell us anything? How did Hurricane Susan affect you?"

"Two trees fell in our yard—a birch and an elm. An oak tree split in half and the elm tree snapped over. Our bridge washed out. And my father let Rain outside during the storm without her collar and she didn't come back."

Parvani gasps. She cranes her neck to look at me and says, "Rain is missing?" Her voice is small.

"Yes," I reply.

"She's been gone since the storm?" asks Josh.

I see Mrs. Kushel and Mrs. Leibler glance at each other. Mrs. Kushel raises her eyebrows, and Mrs. Leibler shrugs her shoulders. It is some kind of conversation.

"That is such a sad story!" Morgan exclaims.

"Yes, it is," I say. Then I add, "I devised a search plan." I tell my classmates about the map and the circles and the lists. "Also, my uncle put an ad in the paper."

"I liked it when Rain came to school," says Josh.

"She's the best dog ever," adds Flo.

"Rose, I hope you find Rain," says Parvani. Now her voice is trembling. She looks at me for so long that I have to turn my eyes away.

Mrs. Kushel touches Parvani's shoulder. "What would you like to share?" she asks gently.

Parvani begins to cry. "My mom is an artist," she tells us. "She stored her paintings in a warehouse and the warehouse flooded and she lost all her work. Everything she's painted for fifteen years."

I stare (stair) at Parvani. I didn't know her mother was an artist. This is very sad.

Tears make wet tracks down Parvani's cheeks. The room grows quiet.

"Parvani?" says Mrs. Kushel. She kneels beside her. Parvani gulps air.

"Do you need to step into the hall?" I ask her.

"Rose—" Mrs. Leibler starts to say.

But Parvani gets to her feet. "Yes," she replies.

Gulping and sobbing and wiping her face with her

sleeve, Parvani winds her way through the desks to the door.

"I'll go with her," I tell Mrs. Leibler, and I follow Parvani into the hall.

Parvani leans her forehead against the wall.

I realize I should say something that will comfort her. "Parvani, I thought of a new homonym this morning. A triple. 'Praise,' 'prays,' and 'preys.' Isn't that good?"

Parvani sniffles and nods her head. "Thank you, Rose."

28
Riding with Uncle Weldon

On the Saturday after school starts again, Uncle Weldon parks his truck on the road in front of our house early in the morning, walks across the plank bridge, and knocks on our door.

"Uncle Weldon's here," I say to my father. "Can I go?"

My uncle and I are ready for a day of searching for Rain. She's been missing for 2 weeks now, which is 14 days, which is not a prime number.

"Let him in," says my father. "I need to talk to him."

I open the door and my uncle and I smile at each other.

"Ready?" Uncle Weldon asks me.

"Ready."

"Just a sec." My father is standing at the sink, drinking orange juice out of the carton. "She needs to be home by five," he says, pointing his thumb at me. "And no spoiling her with treats and ice cream."

"I packed baloney sandwiches," my uncle replies. "They're out in the truck. That's what we're going to eat while Rose spends the day searching for her lost dog."

My father narrows his eyes at his brother. "Is that sarcasm?"

"I'm just stating the facts."

"Unh. All right." My father pauses. "Well, sorry I can't come with you, but I'm going to start working on the permanent bridge today."

I call good-bye to him, and Uncle Weldon and I hurry out to the truck.

"Do you have everything?" he asks me as I climb into my seat.

"Yes." I'm carrying a folder and in it are my lists and the map. Today we're going to drive to the shelters that are closest to Hatford, the ones inside the smallest circle. I've already called all the shelters and been told that no small blond dog with seven white toes has been brought in. But I want to see for myself. Besides, a new dog could come in at any time.

Uncle Weldon studies my list. He thinks for a moment, puts the truck in gear, and says, "Let's go to Rescue Me first, then Furry Friends."

"Furry Friends is where someone called me ma'am," I tell him.

Uncle Weldon laughs. Then he starts driving.

We spend the entire day in the truck or in shelters. Each time we arrive at a shelter we go inside and I step up to the reception desk and say, "Hello. My name is Rose Howard, and this is my uncle, Weldon Howard. We're searching for my dog. She got lost in the storm. I called you before, but I wanted to stop by and look at the dogs."

I have memorized this speech. Uncle Weldon helped me write it last night. It's a lot to say to a stranger, but it's worth it if it will help me find Rain.

Some of the people at the shelters remember talking to me, but some do not, including the MPWWTTAK. I can tell it's the same mean person because I recognize his voice. This time he's nicer, though. Maybe because Uncle Weldon is standing next to me.

After I give my speech, someone at each shelter takes my uncle and me to check the cages of lost or homeless dogs. We look into every cage hoping to see Rain.

We go to four shelters that morning, then we eat

baloney sandwiches in the truck, then we go to six more shelters.

We do not see Rain.

Ten shelters. No (know) Rain (Reign, Rein).

"Time to go home, Rose," says Uncle Weldon as we're leaving the tenth shelter. "I promised your father you'd be back by five."

I'm sitting in (inn) the truck with my chin in (inn) my hand, watching the road (rode, rowed) ahead. I decide not (knot) to (too, two) answer.

"Tired?" asks my uncle.

"Yes."

"Let's get some ice cream."

I slide my eyes to the left. "You promised my father you wouldn't buy me ice cream."

"That was before I knew how hard today would be. Don't you think you deserve a treat?"

"I don't know."

"Can you keep it a secret from your father?"

"Is that like lying?"

"Maybe a little. But sometimes it's all right to reverse our decisions. This morning your father and I decided on no ice cream. But now I think we deserve ice cream after looking at ten shelters and not finding Rain. Okay?"

"Okay." Suddenly I jerk myself upright. "Uncle

Weldon, Uncle Weldon! The lady who's driving that car is talking on her cell phone. That's against the law!"

"Think about ice cream, Rose. Decide what flavor you want."

I close my eyes. "Strawberry," I say.

I don't open my eyes until we reach the Dairy Queen.

29

What Not to Do When You Think of a New Homonym

On Monday the weather is gray and wet. I think that if Rain is still lost outside, she must be cold. Maybe she's shivering.

Mrs. Kushel hands out review sheets for math. One arithmetic problem after another: addition, subtraction, multiplication, and division. I like these sheets. They are very organized. Three columns of ten problems on each sheet.

The problems look easy, so my mind wanders. I start thinking about Rain and then I can't stop thinking about her. This makes me feel sad so I decide to count all the prime numbers on the first page.

"Twenty-three!" I announce to Mrs. Leibler. The room is silent except for my voice. "Twenty-three prime numbers just on this page, and guess what? Twenty-three is a prime number too."

"Rose." Mrs. Leibler looks straight into my eyes and says quietly, "Are you having trouble concentrating? You haven't solved a single problem."

"Yes. I am having trouble concentrating."

"Then let's just take things one at a time. What do you do here?" She taps her fingernail on the first problem in the top row.

I look at it:
$$247$$
$$\underline{\times\,3}$$

I know I'm supposed to multiply the 7 and the 3, but my brain isn't seeing 7 or 3, or 21 either. It's seeing Rain. Rain lost in the rain. Wet and cold and shivering and hungry.

"Rose?" says Mrs. Leibler again. Now she taps my arm with her fingernail. Tap, tap, tap. Her red-painted nail tapping on my skin.

I jerk my arm away.

"Rose?"

"Stop! Stop it!"

I see Mrs. Kushel and Mrs. Leibler glance at each other. Then Mrs. Leibler says, "Time for a break in the hall," and she leads me through the door.

" 'Break' and 'brake' are homonyms," I announce as I slump to the floor.

"Take some time to collect your thoughts," says Mrs. Leibler. "You need a quiet moment."

" 'Time' and 'thyme'—"

Mrs. Leibler puts her finger to her lips. "Shhhh."

I try to control my thoughts. When I feel calmer I say to Mrs. Leibler, "I feel calmer."

"Okay then."

She opens the door and I return to my desk.

Mrs. Kushel leans toward me. "Are you feeling less tense, Rose?" she whispers.

I widen my eyes. "Oh! OH!" I cry. " 'Tense' and 'tents'! That's a brand-new pair of homonyms! A really good one. Thank you, Mrs. Kushel. I have to add those words to my list when I get home. I hope I have space in the *T* section."

I don't want to forget the homonyms, so I tear a sheet of paper from my notebook and carefully write:

tense
tents

I hear snickering. I see Josh Bartel looking at me, then looking at Parvani and rolling his eyes.

Parvani looks away from him, though. She shakes her head. I think that's her way of sticking up for me. I should thank her. I open my mouth, but instead of words what comes out is a wail.

Mrs. Leibler leads me right back into the hall.

If only I knew that Rain would be waiting for me after school.

30

Empty Space

After school, Uncle Weldon drops me at home and goes back to his job.

Here are the things I do in the afternoons now while I wait for my father to come home:

- look through my mother's box
- start my homework
- start dinner

Here are the things I can't do in the afternoons anymore:

- sit on the porch with Rain

- take a walk with Rain
- feed Rain

The afternoons are long. They seem to be full of empty space—space between looking through the box and starting my homework, space between finishing my homework and starting dinner. I don't know what to do with the space. Rain used to fill it.

How do you fill empty space?

31

The Good Phone Call

On the Friday that is three weeks after Hurricane Susan, Uncle Weldon picks me up at school as usual. We are driving along Hud when I notice Sam Diamond's yellow car parked in the road, and then I see my father hauling tools to the bridge.

I wonder why my father is home so early. I thought he was going to be at the J & R Garage all day.

Uncle Weldon stops the truck by the bridge. We cross our fingers and touch our hearts, and then I jump out of the cab and close the door. I turn around and almost run into my father. His eyes are small and mean, and he leans through the window of the truck and says to Uncle Weldon, "That Jerry fired me today." Only instead of the name *Jerry* he uses a word that I'm not allowed to say. "He frickin' fired me," my father goes on. "No reason." He bangs his hands on the side of the truck.

"Whoa," says my uncle. "What are you going to do?"

"Finish the bridge."

"And then what?"

"I don't know 'and then what' right now, okay?"

"But shouldn't you think ahead a little? You can't just live day to day." Uncle Weldon looks like he has something more to say, but my father interrupts him.

"I got plenty to do around here. The yard's still a mess. I'll keep busy."

"That's not what I meant."

I run around to Uncle Weldon's side of the truck, stand on my toes, and whisper to him, "What about money?"

"Rose, I can see you, you know," says my father through the truck. "I can hear you too. You think I can't support us? I can support us. Now go on inside."

I cross the bridge as fast as I can. Behind me I hear Uncle Weldon clear his throat and say, "Rose does have a point, Wesley. What *are* you going to do for money? Rose needs new clothes—"

My father bangs the truck with his fists again. "Don't tell me what Rose needs." He's yelling with his hands instead of his voice.

That's the end of the conversation. I don't hear anything but the sound of the truck starting up as I dash onto the porch, pass the empty couch, and hurry into the house.

I take the telephone into my room and throw my school bag on the floor. Then I get out my lists of shelters. I have called every single shelter on all the lists, but I've only called the farthest shelters, the ones in the widest ring on the map, once. It's time to call them again. Just in case. Just in case Rain got washed very far away. Or in case her nose wasn't working well and she wandered in the wrong direction.

I call Boonton Animal Rescue Center. Still no Rain.

I call Safe Haven Shelter. Still no Rain.

I call Olivebridge Animal Adoption Network. Still no Rain.

Then I call Happy Tails Animal Shelter. A voice answers the phone and when I determine that it's the voice of a real person, not a recorded voice, I say, "Hello, this is Rose again. I called last week. I'm still looking for my dog, Rain. She got lost during the storm. She has yellow fur and seven white toes. Has anyone brought her in?"

The person on the other end of the line, who is a man, says, "How big is she? Do you know how much she weighs?"

"She weighs twenty-three pounds," I reply. I remind myself not to add that 23 is a prime number. That is not appropriate for this conversation.

"And she has white toes?"

"They're not all white," I say. "Just seven are. Two on her right front paw, one on her left front paw, three on her right back paw, and one on her left back paw."

"Hang on a sec." I can hear the man talking to someone. He's repeating the information about Rain's toes. Then he says to me, "Hang on just a few more seconds, okay?"

There's a long silence. I look out my window. I think about homonyms: toe/tow and toes/tows.

Finally I hear a voice in my ear again. "We do have a dog like that here," says the man. He sounds excited. "Someone brought her in several days ago. A young blond female dog with seven white toes, just like you described. We've been trying to—"

My hands start to shake. I drop the phone and it rolls onto the floor. I can't think. I put my hands over my ears and jump up and down on my bed. Then I jump off the bed and pick up the phone. I can hear the man saying, "Hello? Hello?" I click the phone off. Then I click it on again. I dial Uncle Weldon's number before I remember that he's still on his way back to work. I click the phone off. I get out the map and draw a large red circle around Elmara, New York, where Happy Tails is located. I sit on my hands and try to remember every single thing that's in my mother's box. Finally I phone my uncle again.

He answers on the first ring. "Everything all right?" he asks.

"Rain might be in Elmara!" I cry. "There's a blond dog with seven white toes at the shelter. Someone brought her in a few days ago. Can we go to Elmara, please? Please?"

"I'll pick you up tomorrow morning at nine o'clock," says my uncle.

32

The Happy Tails Animal Shelter in Elmara, New York

By 8:45 the next morning I am sitting on our porch, just in case Uncle Weldon arrives early. He arrives at 8:55, and I jump up from the couch, call good-bye to my father, and run across our yard to the truck.

Uncle Weldon and I are in a good mood on the drive to Elmara. We talk about homonyms and prime numbers, and I tell him about Parvani's mother. "Parvani cries a lot at school," I add. "I think she's very sad. I cheer her up with homonyms."

The closer we get to Elmara, the more I talk.

"Uncle Weldon! Uncle Weldon! There's a sign for Happy Tails Animal Shelter! 'Tails' has a homonym. 'Tales.' That's a good sign, isn't it? Isn't it a good sign? I think it is. I'm sure Rain is the 23-pound blond dog with the seven white toes that someone brought in. Both 23 and 7 are prime numbers."

"Rose." My uncle interrupts me. "Don't get too excited. Just in case."

"Just in case what?"

"Just in case the blond dog with white toes isn't Rain after all. Okay?"

"Okay," I say. But I'm bouncing up and down in my seat, feeling happy.

Uncle Weldon puts on his directional, and we turn left and rumble along a dirt road. I see a sign that says HAPPY TAILS—JUST AHEAD. Soon the road ends in a parking lot by a long low building. Now I see a bigger sign that says HAPPY TAILS. Under the words are a painting of a dog and a cat curled up together, their tails entwined.

"Where do we park? Where do we park?" I cry.

"Rose, calm down," says my uncle. "Here's a parking space. And over there I see a sign that says OFFICE. Let's go."

I run ahead of my uncle, through the parking lot,

and along a walk to the OFFICE sign. I pull open a door. Inside I see a waiting room with a desk and a lot of hard plastic chairs. Some of the chairs are occupied. Most of them are empty. I don't pay any attention to the people in the chairs. I'm only interested in the man behind the desk.

"Rose, slow down!" my uncle calls after me, but he's laughing.

I step up to the desk, stand on tiptoes, and say to the man, "My name is Rose Howard. I called yesterday about my dog."

I explain about Rain again, and the man begins to smile. "Yes," he says. "We were hoping you would come in. Just a moment. Let me get the shelter manager."

He speaks into a phone on the desk and a few minutes later a door at the back of the room opens and a woman walks through it. She's holding a leash and saying, "Come on. Come on, girl."

I watch the leash as it follows the woman through the door, watch and watch, until finally I can see what's at the other end.

"Rain!" I cry.

I run to her. Rain seems confused at first. Her eyes dart around the room as she looks at the strange people. But then they settle on Uncle Weldon and me, and she begins to leap and jump and yip and bark.

I slide onto my knees and throw my arms around Rain. She wiggles so hard that her entire body vibrates. Then she puts her front paws on my shoulders and licks my face.

"Rain," I say again. I look behind me at Uncle Weldon. "It's really her," I whisper.

I see that my uncle is crying. Then I see that the woman with the leash is crying, and so is the man behind the desk, and so are two of the people sitting in the hard plastic chairs.

Tears are running down my own face, but Rain licks them away, so I don't have to worry about them.

When Rain and I finally settle down and everyone has stopped crying, the shelter manager holds out her hand to Uncle Weldon and says, "My name is Julie Caporale."

Uncle Weldon and Julie Caporale talk for a while. I don't pay much attention to what they're saying. I sit on the floor where Rain has climbed into my lap and I stroke her ears and paws, and examine her closely. She looks thin, and she has some cuts on her face and some marks on her belly that might be insect bites. But she is still my Rain.

After a long time I hear Mrs. Caporale say to my uncle, "It's clear that this lucky pup has found her owners, but I have to follow procedure before we release her to you. Could you please show me some identification? I need to make sure that the information on your ID matches the information on the microchip. I'm a little confused because the chip says the dog's name is Olivia, not Rain."

I twist my head around to look at Uncle Weldon.

"I'll be happy to show you my driver's license," he says, "but I should tell you that I'm Rose's uncle, not her father, and—"

I have to interrupt the conversation.

"What's a microchip?" I ask.

33

What a Microchip Is

It turns out that a microchip is a tiny chip, about the size of a grain of rice, that a veterinarian injects into a pet, and that contains information such as who the pet's owners are and how to contact them.

"We scanned Olivia—excuse me, Rain—for a chip when she was brought in," Mrs. Caporale tells Uncle Weldon and me.

She's been talking for a long time now, explaining microchip technology, and I'm trying hard not to interrupt again, but finally I can't help it. "We didn't have Rain microchipped!" I burst out. "We've never even taken her to the vet."

"But she does have a microchip," says Mrs. Caporale.

"Are you sure?" I'm getting a strange feeling in my stomach.

"Of course. We scanned it, and that's how we know her name is Olivia." Mrs. Caporale is frowning now. She sits in one of the chairs and opens a folder she's been carrying. Then she turns to Uncle Weldon. "So you aren't Jason Henderson? From Gloverstown?"

Uncle Weldon shakes his head.

"We've been trying to contact the Hendersons, but we haven't had any luck," says Mrs. Caporale. "That's why we were so pleased when you called yesterday, Rose—even though you hung up before we could get your number. Our phones have been misbehaving ever since the storm," she adds, and smiles at me. "We thought you were one of the Hendersons. We assumed they'd had to move because of Susan. Gloverstown got hit badly and we just get a fast busy signal whenever we call the Hendersons' home number. And they didn't include a cell number on their contact information, so . . ." She spreads her hands.

I slump onto the floor with Rain again. I put my arms around her and feel her fur against my neck. She's so soft that I think maybe she's been given a bath recently. I rest my cheek next to her face.

"Who are you, Rain?" I whisper.

34

What Mrs. Caporale Says

Mrs. Caporale and Uncle Weldon continue their conversation. I sit on the floor and think about Rain and my father.

I remember the night my father brought Rain home. I wonder if my father didn't know about microchips or if he just didn't want to look for Rain's owners.

I think of my father letting Rain outside during a superstorm without her collar.

I realize that my father hasn't helped me one bit in my search for Rain.

I turn around and say to Mrs. Caporale, "My father found Rain in the rain. That's why I named her Rain.

Also, it's a homonym." (Mrs. Caporale looks puzzled.) "Rain was all by herself with no collar," I continue.

"Did you try to look for her owners?" Mrs. Caporale asks.

I shake my head. "My father said we couldn't look because she didn't have any identification. Also, he said if she had owners they must not have cared very much about her." I pause and then say in a smaller voice, "But they cared enough to have her microchipped."

Mrs. Caporale looks at me and says gently, "Pets can get separated from their owners for all kinds of reasons. Getting lost or separated doesn't mean the owners are irresponsible."

I wonder if Mrs. Caporale is talking about the Hendersons or about my father and me.

I nod. For some reason, I feel like crying again, so I say, "Two, three, five, seven, eleven." But I say it in my head so that I'm the only one who hears it.

I see Uncle Weldon look from Rain and me to Mrs. Caporale. "What happens now?" he asks. "Do we leave Rain here?"

"No!" I cry. (No, no, know, know.) I jump to my feet.

Rain stands up too, looking nervous. She leans against my legs and nuzzles my hand with her nose (knows).

Mrs. Caporale lets out a breath of air that puffs her

hair away from her forehead. "This is the first time I've run into this situation," she admits. "Let me talk to one of my co-workers."

She leaves the waiting room. Uncle Weldon and I sit in the chairs. Rain jumps up and settles herself with her head in my lap and her rear in Uncle Weldon's lap.

I say to my uncle, "I'd feel better if Olivia was a homonym name, but it isn't."

Uncle Weldon gives me a sad smile.

At last Mrs. Caporale returns. She sits next to Uncle Weldon and says, "See if you think this is fair: Considering that we've been trying to reach the Hendersons and haven't had any luck, and considering that Rain has been living with Rose for a year and clearly loves her—"

"And I love Rain," I say.

"—and you love Rain," Mrs. Caporale continues, "we've decided that she should go home with you, at least temporarily. It only seems fair, and she'll certainly be happier living with you than living here at the shelter."

"Thank you!" I cry.

"However," Mrs. Caporale goes on, "we will continue to search for the Hendersons. We're busier than usual just now, because of the storm, but we will search.

And if we reach them, or if they contact us, and they want Rain back, well then . . ." She spreads her hands again. "Rain is their dog after all. I mean, she was. Originally. So, please fill out this form with your information and we'll keep it on file." She starts to hand the form to me, then looks at Uncle Weldon.

"I'll fill it out," he says. "I'll put down my information as well as Rose's and her father's."

Five minutes later Uncle Weldon and I are walking out of Happy Tails with Rain between us.

IV

The Hard Part

35

The Thing I Have to Do

When Uncle Weldon and I park on Hud Road by the plank bridge over the stream and climb out of the truck with Rain, my father, who is working in the yard, gets a look on his face that is most likely surprise. His eyes grow big and at first he doesn't say anything.

Uncle Weldon takes my hand and we start across the bridge, Rain ahead of us. She picks her way slowly because she isn't used to balancing on the planks. When she reaches our yard she catches sight of my father, standing among lots of tools and boards. She gives a little wag of her tail.

Finally my father speaks. He says, "Well, I'll be."

I'm not sure what that means. I say, "We found Rain."

"Yes. I see that."

"Do you feel happy?" I ask my father.

He kneels down as Rain trots closer to him. "I'm just surprised, that's all. I can't believe you found her."

So I was right about feeling surprised.

"I had a plan," I remind him. "It was a good plan."

"I guess so," says my father, who is patting Rain.

"Except," says Uncle Weldon from behind me, "there's . . . an issue."

My father looks up sharply, and then he gets to his feet. "An issue?"

Uncle Weldon explains about the Hendersons and the microchip.

I look closely at my father when Uncle Weldon says "microchip." My father is frowning.

"Rain had identification after all," I point out.

Now my father looks sharply at me. "What are you saying?"

I think for a moment. "I said that Rain had identification after all."

My father shakes his head. "Look, you got your dog back, Rose. Just let it be."

On the ride home from Happy Tails, Rain sat in my lap. She barely moved, and she kept her face pressed next to my cheek so that I could feel her whiskers and little puffs of air as she breathed. Every now and then she turned and licked my nose.

I look around the yard. My father and I have cleaned it up pretty well. My father is working on the permanent bridge, and as long as we have the temporary one we aren't stranded on our property anymore. Our power and phones are back, and school has started again. Most important of all, Rain is home.

I know I should feel happiness. If Parvani's mother somehow got all her artwork back safe and sound, she would feel happiness. But I don't feel happiness. Instead, I feel that something is wrong.

I thank Uncle Weldon for helping me, and Rain and I go into the house. Rain sniffs at everything on the way—twigs, logs, weeds, the porch steps, the couch on the porch. Then she sniffs her way through the house and into my room where she jumps on the bed and looks at me. I sit next to her and wrap my arms around her neck.

Then, because something still feels wrong, I start to cry. I cry into Rain's fur and she sits there patiently, occasionally turning to lick my cheeks, until I get a Kleenex and blow my nose and make the tears stop.

I know what is wrong. It's what my father said a few minutes ago: "You got your dog back, Rose."

Your dog back. *Your* dog back, Rose.

But Rain isn't my dog. Rain is the Hendersons' dog. She belongs to them. Or she used to. And they cared enough about her to have her microchipped. I don't know how she got separated from them, but she did, and they probably want her back. Especially now. Especially if they've lost their home in the storm and are feeling very, very sad.

I know what I have to do.

I don't want to do it, but rules are rules, and I must follow them.

Somewhere a family named Henderson is missing Rain. If they miss her as much as I missed her when she was lost, then they want her badly. And she belongs to them. I don't know when the shelter will start their search for the Hendersons, but I need to start mine now.

I have to find the Hendersons and give Rain back.

Rain lets out a sigh and flops on my bed. I lie down beside her. I wonder if she knows what I'm thinking.

I recall the information on Rain's microchip form. Mrs. Caporale didn't give the information to Uncle Weldon, but I peeked at the form and saw the Hendersons' phone number and address and memorized them. I know where they live, or where they used to live. The information will help in my new search.

I do some mental calculations. The name Henderson comes out to 102, which is clearly not a prime number. Olivia is not a prime number name either.

I don't know if this means anything.

36

Mrs. Kushel's Helpful Suggestions

Ever since the storm Mrs. Kushel has started off each morning in class by asking if anyone has anything they'd like to share. For fifteen minutes, we raise our hands and tell our classmates about things that are troubling us, or things that are getting better. The Monday after Uncle Weldon and I bring Rain home, I say to my classmates, "Rain is back. We found her at the Happy Tails Animal Shelter in Elmara, New York."

Everyone has questions. "Is she okay?" "Did she remember you?" "Was she happy to see you?" "How did she get all the way to Elmara?" "Why didn't she follow her nose back to your house?"

I answer the questions as well as I can.

I do not mention the Hendersons or the microchip.

I am privately working on my new plan. I called the Hendersons' phone number, but just like Mrs. Caporale said, all I got was a strange busy signal. So I'm not sure how to look for the Hendersons. But I know someone I can ask for advice.

One morning Uncle Weldon agrees to take me to school ten minutes earlier than usual. I arrive before Mrs. Leibler does, and so I walk to my classroom by myself. I find Mrs. Kushel sitting at her desk. No one else is in the room.

"Mrs. Kushel?" I say.

She jumps a little. "Rose! You're here early."

I stare at her. "I have a question."

Mrs. Kushel puts her pen down and looks at me very seriously. "Yes?"

"How would someone who found a lost dog look for the owners of the dog?"

"Well, the person could place an ad in the newspaper," Mrs. Kushel replies, "and also check the paper for ads about lost dogs. He could put up posters with a picture of the dog and information about when and where

169

the dog was found. Also, he could call vets and shelters and put up posts on Web sites for lost pets."

"Mm-hmm," I say.

Mrs. Kushel frowns at me. "Did you find a lost dog, Rose?"

I nod my head. "Yes."

37

Where Rain Used to Live

Secretly, at times when my father is not in the house, I phone the Hendersons' number. Each time I get the fast busy signal. It's not the same kind of busy signal I get when I call Uncle Weldon and he's on the phone. Most people have Call Waiting now, and you don't get a busy signal at all when you dial them. But maybe the Hendersons are like Uncle Weldon and don't have Call Waiting. Still, their busy signal sounds strange. I decide that their phone is out of order.

For this reason, I feel grateful that Mrs. Kushel is going to help me with posters. She said she'll put an ad in the paper for me too, and on some of the Web sites about lost and found pets.

We run into a problem right away, though. This is the conversation in which I realize the problem:

MRS. KUSHEL: Now, the first thing you must do is take a picture of the dog you found. A picture is even better than describing the dog.

ROSE HOWARD: A picture?

MRS. KUSHEL: Yes. Can you do that?

I can but I don't want to. I don't want Mrs. Kushel to see that the picture is of Rain.

I nod my head.

MRS. KUSHEL: Good. Now, under the picture we should write "Found" and then you can describe the dog.

ROSE HOWARD: Even though there's a picture of the dog right there?

MRS. KUSHEL: Yes. You can give a few more details, such as the dog's approximate age and weight, and also where you found the dog.

ROSE HOWARD: Oh.

I decide that maybe we should wait a bit before we put up posters of Rain. I'm not ready to explain things to Mrs. Kushel.

But I am ready to tell my new plan to Uncle Weldon. I call him one night and say, "I think we need to look for the Hendersons."

"Who?" he asks.

"Rain's real owners. It's only right. And only fair. Rules are rules: No name-calling. Put away the math game when you aren't using it because someone who finished her worksheets might be waiting for it. And—"

Uncle Weldon interrupts me. "And make sure Rain's original owners get their dog back."

"Yes," I say.

"Oh, Rose. Are you sure you want to do this?"

"We practically stole her," I reply in a small voice.

"Now don't get carried away."

I'm patting Rain while we talk. "I'm not carried away." I add, "I have another plan."

I tell Uncle Weldon that I secretly know the Hendersons' address in Gloverstown. "We could start by looking for their house. Maybe they still live there but their phone is just out of order after the storm."

We decide to go to Gloverstown the next day, which is Saturday. We get an early start. My father is barely out of bed. We leave him sitting at the kitchen table in his underwear, muttering and grunting and calling the people at the J & R Garage bad names.

Gloverstown is about thirty miles from Hatford in the opposite direction from Elmara.

"It's one of the towns that got hit the worst by Susan," Uncle Weldon comments as we drive along. "I don't think there's much left of it."

He's right. When we reach what used to be the main street through Gloverstown we see that it now looks like a dried-up riverbed. And everything on either side of it is ruined and abandoned. Wooden porches droop and dip, their railings missing. The sidewalks are gone, and broken store windows have been patched with tape, but carelessly, as if the owners don't expect to be able to salvage their businesses. We don't see a single person.

Uncle Weldon skirts around the town and finally we come across the road where the Hendersons live. It's a lonely country road and we don't see any houses, although we see a lot of storm damage. Finally we spot a mailbox with the excellent prime number 2 painted on the side.

"That's it!" I say.

Uncle Weldon turns onto a gravel drive and we creep along, avoiding potholes and tree limbs.

We round a bend. "Whoa," says Uncle Weldon under his breath.

The house that once stood there, Rain's old home, is

now a pile of lumber and rubble, surrounded by fallen trees.

We get out of the car and listen to the country sounds of branches rustling and birds chirping.

Uncle Weldon calls, "Hello?"

No one answers.

We get in the car and drive back toward town.

38

The General Store in Gloverstown

"Do you think they're all right?" I ask Uncle Weldon as we drive along.

"The Hendersons? I don't know. I hope they went to a shelter before the storm hit."

"How will we find them?" I ask.

Uncle Weldon shakes his head. "Let me think about this."

We drive back to Gloverstown, past the end of the ruined main street, and are about to turn onto Route 28, when I say, "Hey!"

A little country store sits by the side of the road. It

looks just like a house—a white house with black shutters, a wide front porch, and a brick chimney. But a sign above the door reads GENERAL STORE.

"Can we stop here?" I ask.

"Sure. Are you hungry?"

"No. I have an idea."

Uncle Weldon follows me inside. The store is crammed with shelf after shelf of everything you can think of: nails, board games, cans of soup, T-shirts, batteries, aspirin, cereal, Band-Aids, pens, candy bars, thread, socks.

"Can I help you?"

Standing behind the counter is a young man wearing overalls and a flannel shirt.

My heart starts to pound, but I step up to the counter anyway, and I say, "My name is Rose Howard and I'm looking for the Hendersons who used to live at number two Slide Road."

The man frowns and I think maybe he's going to ask why I want to find the Hendersons. Instead he says, "Henderson, Henderson. Jason and Carol Henderson? And a couple of little kids?"

I remember the names Jason and Carol from the microchip information, so I say, "Yes."

"Didn't know them well."

"*Didn't* know them?"

"They had to move away after the storm. Too much damage to their house."

I let out a breath. So they're still alive.

"Do you know where they went?" I ask.

The man shakes his head. "No. But they have relatives somewhere around here. Maybe they're staying with them."

"Okay." I glare into the man's eyes and say, "Thank you."

Uncle Weldon and I are on our way out of the store when I see a rack of newspapers, including one called *The County Gazette*. I point to a copy. "Uncle Weldon? Could we buy that?"

"Sure. But why?"

"If we put an ad in it, maybe the Hendersons will see it."

39
Found:
Blond Female Dog

Halloween came and went, and now Thanksgiving comes and goes. My father and Rain and I have a turkey dinner at Uncle Weldon's house. Over the weekend I think a lot about the Hendersons. I decide that I must tell Mrs. Kushel the truth about Rain. So on Monday I ask my uncle if he can drop me off at school early again. It's time for another private conversation with my teacher.

I enter our classroom and find Mrs. Kushel working on a new bulletin board. She's tacking up large colorful letters that spell HOLIDAYS.

"Good morning, Rose," she says.

"Good morning," I reply, looking her in the eye.

Mrs. Kushel steps off the chair she's been standing on. "Is there something you'd like to talk about?" she asks. "Did you bring the photo of the dog you found?"

She has asked two questions in a row. I answer the first one. "There is something I'd like to talk about."

I sit at my desk and Mrs. Kushel sits next to me in Mrs. Leibler's chair.

"I have to tell you something," I say. "I have to tell you the truth."

Mrs. Kushel smiles at me, which is a sign of encouragement.

"The truth is that the lost dog is Rain."

Mrs. Kushel's smile turns to a frown. "I don't understand."

I tell my teacher the whole story of Rain, starting from the night my father brought her home and said we couldn't look for her owners if she didn't have any identification.

"So Rain is back," I finish up. "But she isn't my dog, and we have to find her real owners—the Hendersons who used to live in Gloverstown, whose house got ruined, and who might be living nearby with relatives."

Just like Uncle Weldon, Mrs. Kushel says to me, "Oh, Rose. Are you sure?"

I nod my head. "Yes. I am sure. It's the right thing to do. Happy Tails is looking for her owners too."

Mrs. Kushel frowns again, and taps a pencil on the edge of my desk. This is an indication that she's thinking. She says, "I have an idea. Instead of placing an ad in the paper, maybe someone could write an article. An article would get a lot of attention, certainly more attention than a little ad.

"I'll have to ask your father for permission, of course," Mrs. Kushel continues. She sounds as though she's talking to herself. "Then I'll call a friend of mine, Sheila Perlman, who's a writer. She'll write a good story, and it would probably be picked up by lots of the local papers. How do you feel about this, Rose?"

"I feel that it's a good idea."

"I'll call your father tonight."

"Maybe you should call him in the afternoon," I say, thinking of all the time my father has been spending at The Luck of the Irish lately. The earlier she talks to him, the less chance there is that he will have had a drink already.

"Deal," says Mrs. Kushel.

• • •

Three days later I arrive at school wearing the same dress I wore on school picture day. My hair is brushed and Uncle Weldon tied a ribbon in it.

When it's time for recess, my classmates leave the cafeteria and run to the playground, while Mrs. Kushel and I walk back to our room. Waiting there is a woman wearing a blue wool jacket and matching blue wool pants. Her face looks serious, but when she sees me she smiles.

"Rose," says Mrs. Kushel, "meet Ms. Perlman. She's the writer. Ms. Perlman, this is Rose Howard."

Ms. Perlman stretches out her hand and I know I'm supposed to shake it, which I do.

"Well," says my teacher, "shall we get down to business?"

Ms. Perlman opens a laptop computer. She starts asking me questions—questions about Rain, about when my father brought her home, about how we lost her and how we found her. And then more questions about what happened after we located her at Happy Tails. I give her a photo of Rain that Uncle Weldon took with his digital camera.

Ms. Perlman looks at the photo, looks at me, looks at the photo again, and when she glances at me a second time I think I see tears in her eyes. "This is a very brave and selfless thing you're doing, Rose," she says. "Giving up the dog you love so that her proper owners can be reunited with her."

I nod. Maybe I'm supposed to say thank you.

Two, three, five, seven, eleven.

When I say nothing, Ms. Perlman says to Mrs. Kushel, "At the end of the article we'll include a contact number—a number at the *Hatford Herald*—that people can call if they have any information about Rain or the Hendersons. That way Rose's personal information will remain private."

Mrs. Kushel nods. "I'll explain that to Rose's fa—" She pauses. "I think I'll explain it to her uncle, when he picks her up today."

Ms. Perlman turns to me and smiles. "That about wraps things up. Thank you very much, Rose."

"You're very welcome, Ms. Perlman," I reply, and stick out my hand so she can shake it again.

40

Parvani Finds a Homonym

We are writing compositions in Mrs. Kushel's class. Christmas and Hanukkah are almost here, but when Mrs. Kushel asked what we would like to write about, every single one of us said, "Hurricane Susan." We are not finished thinking about our ruined homes and wrecked artwork, our washed-away bridges and lost dogs.

I don't know exactly what the subject of Parvani's composition is, but suddenly she shoots her hand in the air and says, "Mrs. Kushel? What's that word you taught us that means to tear something down?"

Mrs. Kushel puts on her thoughtful face and taps her pencil against her fingers. "Raze?" she suggests after a moment.

"Yes!" exclaims Parvani. And then she can't help herself. She jumps out of her seat, runs to my desk, and cries, "Rose, I thought of a triple homonym—'raze,' 'raise,' and 'rays'!"

I have thought of that triple homonym before, but I know this is not the time to mention it. Instead, this is the time for the feeling of friendliness. Since a friend would probably not say, "I already thought of that," I grin at Parvani and exclaim, "That's a great one!" I put enthusiasm into my voice.

Parvani places her palm in the air. "High-five," she says.

I give her a high five, and then we go back to our compositions. We are both smiling.

41

My Father Makes a Mistake with Pronouns

"What is this?" My father is asking the question. (This is not when he makes a mistake with pronouns.) He's holding out a newspaper.

Uncle Weldon has just dropped me off after school, and I'm walking through the front door, Rain at my side because she's been waiting for me on the porch.

"It's a newspaper," I say.

My father's face is hard and there's no smile on it. "Of course it's a *news*paper," he replies. He throws it at my feet. "Sam Diamond gave it to me this morning. He said there was something in it that I would want to see. He was right. Is there anything you want to tell me?"

I feel confused, but more than that, I feel frightened. "No," I say.

My father picks the paper up and turns the pages so fiercely that they rip in his hands. He turns the pages three times and then he stops and shoves one of them at me. "What is this?"

It's the second time he's asked that question.

I look at the page. I see a picture of Rain. And an article—a long one—titled "A Girl's Brave Search." The author of the article is Sheila Perlman.

"It's the article Mrs. Kushel called you about," I tell my father.

"Nobody called me about any article."

I hand the paper back to him. "Mrs. Kushel did."

My father pauses for a long time and his eyes wander around the room. I know he's suddenly remembering the afternoon when he came home from The Luck of the Irish and the phone rang. He picked it up and said hello, and then he frowned and the next thing he said was, "What did Rose do? Is she in trouble again?" He put his hand over the mouthpiece and whispered to me, "It's Mrs. Kushel."

"Okay," I said.

My father reached for the remote control and aimed it at the television. He pressed the Mute button and flicked silently through channels. Every now and then he said "Unh" or "Uh-huh" into the phone. Eventually, he hung up. "What did you tell your teacher about Rain for?" he asked me before he turned the volume back on.

Now my father shakes his head. "This is our private business, Rose. Our private family business. And now it's all over the paper. Everyone in the county will read this. I look like a thief."

I back away. Rain backs away too. She does not take her eyes off my father. "Talk to Uncle Weldon," I say. I know my uncle hasn't had time to return to his office yet, but I don't want my father to call Mrs. Kushel and yell at her. "I need to take Rain for a walk," I add. "Let's call Uncle Weldon when I get back."

I hustle Rain outside and we walk up and down the street until I think Uncle Weldon is at his desk at work. Then we cross the planks into our yard again.

My father is sitting at the kitchen table, doing nothing. I pick up the phone and dial Uncle Weldon's number. I tell him what's happened and he says, "Let me speak to your father, please."

I feel a little mad at my father now, so I stand by the table, staring at him and listening to his end of the conversation. At first he doesn't say much, but then he shouts, "*Okay!* I won't phone anyone. I won't make any trouble." He hangs up without saying good-bye to Uncle Weldon. Then he looks at me. "Sit down, Rose."

I don't want to sit near my father. "Where?" I say.

My father kicks a chair away from the table. "Right there."

I perch on the edge of the chair.

"Why are you doing this, Rose? Why are you looking for Rain's owners? She was my gift to you. My *gift*. Not to mention that you got her twice. Once from me and once from the shelter. You should count your lucky stars."

"But if you hadn't let Rain out during a superstorm," I say, "I wouldn't have had to get her back." I look down at Rain, then up at my father again. "Why did you let her outside during the storm?"

"Rose, for the love of Pete." I see color rising in my father's face.

"But why did you? Rain had never been outside during a storm before. Not by herself."

When my father speaks again his voice is very low, but not in a gentle way like when Mrs. Kushel reads to our class. It's a different kind of low. "You should count your lucky stars and your blessings, Rose. You have your frickin' dog back."

This is not logical. "I wouldn't have had to get

her back if you hadn't let her out. Why did you let her out?"

My father slams his hand down on the table so suddenly and so hard that Rain and I jump. "Look, you little brat. I brought that home for you." He points to Rain. "I was trying to do something nice."

"Rain is a 'she,'" I inform him, "not a 'that.'"

My father gets to his feet and stands over me.

42

Protecting Rain

"What did you say?" my father asks.

I shake my head. He's so much bigger than I am. I hadn't noticed. I hadn't noticed how thick and hard his hands are, how wide his shoulders are.

Two, three, five, seven.

"Answer me," my father says in that same low voice.

I slip off the edge of my chair and sidestep toward my bedroom.

"Come here."

"No."

"All right." My father takes two giant steps toward me, his arm raised, his fingers clenched into a fist. I can see each white knuckle, as hard as a stone.

He's never raised his fist to me. Not once that I remember. This is because of not wanting to be the kind of father that his father was.

I'm looking from my bedroom door to the front door, trying to decide which one is closer, when a blur of blond fur hurtles into the air and leaps against my father's chest, growling.

"Rain!" I cry.

She lands on the floor and gets ready to spring again, but before she can, my father lowers his fist. He brings it down on Rain's back and she lurches sideways and crashes into the legs of the table. I hear a crunch, and Rain's yelp of fear and pain.

I turn and fling myself beneath the table so fast I skin my knees on the floorboards. I gather Rain into my arms and slide us under the very center of the table. My father reaches for us and I scoot us away from his grasp, again and again, like we are targets in a game.

"Don't touch her!" I cry. "Do not touch her, do not hurt her."

I won't let go of Rain. After a few moments the hand disappears. I hear footsteps crossing the room to the front door. The knob begins to turn, then stops. I slide forward a few inches and peer out from under the table.

"If you say one word about this to anyone,

Rose—*one word*—" My father is breathing heavily. He has to pause before he can continue speaking. "If you say one word to Weldon, to Mrs. Kushel—" His gaze drifts to Rain who, although she's trembling, has also poked her head out from under the table. He glares at her. He doesn't finish his sentence. He doesn't have to. I slide Rain behind me so that she's out of his sight.

My father grabs his keys and slams the front door behind him. I hold Rain for a long time. We're breathing heavily too. My breath comes in gasps, and Rain pants and drools.

When I hear Sam Diamond's car start up, I crawl out from under the table. I pull Rain after me and we sit on the couch. I pat her whole body, over and over. Nothing seems to hurt her. I make her walk across the floor. She doesn't limp.

Later I feed Rain her dinner. I walk her earlier than usual, even though this is an unwelcome change in our schedule, and then I close her into my room.

I wonder how I'll be able to protect her when I'm at school.

• • •

I'm still up when my father comes home. I'm sitting in the living room with the TV on.

My father stands before me and says, "I'm sorry, Rose. It won't happen again."

I look into his eyes. I don't know how to read what I see there, so I say nothing.

"Really," my father continues. "I'm very sorry. Very, very sorry."

"Okay," I say.

This may be a sincere apology.

43

What Mrs. Kushel Says

Time passes in school the way it always does. Mrs. Kushel changes the bulletin board from HOLIDAYS to WE ARE ALL ARTISTS! Some of the snow melts and for a while the playground is muddy and wet instead of snowy and wet. The next holiday will be Martin Luther King Jr. Day.

On a morning that is dark and rainy and chilly, Mrs. Leibler walks me to our classroom as usual. But something that is not usual is that Mrs. Kushel takes me to the back of the room as soon as I have hung up my coat and put my things in my desk.

"I want to speak with you privately, Rose," she says.

I wonder if I have done something that she and Mrs. Leibler will write about in the weekly note to my father.

"Okay," I say, and think about homonyms. *Tied* and *tide* is a new one.

"I wanted to let you know that the newspaper got a call about Rain yesterday."

Tied, tide. Died, dyed.

"Are you listening to me, Rose?"

"Yes."

"A man named Jason Henderson phoned. He said someone had just sent him the article and that Rain is his family's dog. The newspaper put him in touch with Happy Tails, and Mrs. Caporale is certain that he and his family are Rain's original owners. All their information matches up with the information from Rain's chip. Also, they have lots of photos of themselves with Rain." Mrs. Kushel pauses and looks at me seriously. "I don't know whether this is good news for you or bad news."

"The article worked," I say.

"Yes, it did. Would you like to know how Rain got separated from the Hendersons?"

"Yes."

"They always took her collar off when she was in the house so that it wouldn't get snagged on anything. One day the Hendersons went out and left Rain at home alone. A neighbor dropped by to leave something in their kitchen and Rain slipped outside without her collar.

The neighbor didn't see her leave, so it was several hours before anyone knew she was missing. This happened two days before your father found her, Rose."

"The Hendersons weren't irresponsible after all," I say. "It was an accident." Rain left their house without her collar, just like she left our house after the storm without her collar.

"Yes. A sad accident. We'll never know how Rain wound up so far from home, but she did. The Hendersons looked for her in their town—they put up flyers and placed an ad in the paper—but no one called to say they had found her."

"Because we had her."

Mrs. Kushel cocks her head to the side. "But now you've done a very brave thing, like Ms. Perlman said."

"Okay."

"The rest of the story you learned yourself. The Hendersons had to abandon their home after the storm, and they're living with relatives now. That's why it was so hard to locate them." Mrs. Kushel pauses. "They want Rain back, Rose. They love her and miss her and want her very badly."

"Okay."

44

Good-bye

The very next day Uncle Weldon picks me up from school, as usual. He drives me home, as usual. When we reach our house, I cross the planks as usual, and I see Rain watching me from a window. What is not usual is that Uncle Weldon is still sitting in the truck. He's waiting for Rain and me.

I put my school things inside. Then I clip Rain's leash to her collar and walk her around the yard for a while. She pees and poops, and sniffs at her favorite things—a stump, the bottom porch step, a particular spot near the garage door. Uncle Weldon watches us from the truck.

My father is not at home. He's probably at The Luck

of the Irish. But I can tell that he was working on the new bridge this morning.

I think my father doesn't want to say good-bye to Rain.

I lead Rain to the truck. She sits between Uncle Weldon and me as we drive along. She looks out the window seriously.

The other day Mrs. Leibler told me to try to see things from someone else's perspective. "Put yourself in that person's place, Rose," she said. "What do you think she's thinking? What is she feeling?" I'm not sure what Rain is thinking or feeling now, but she looks like she's watching the road for people who are making driving mistakes.

Uncle Weldon and Rain and I ride to Happy Tails. We don't say much. Our space in the truck is very quiet.

I stroke the white toes on Rain's front feet. Her toes are as soft as pussy willows.

Uncle Weldon turns onto the drive to Happy Tails. He parks the truck and then he looks at me for a long time.

"Are you all right, Rose?" he asks.

I stare out the window and remember my father whacking Rain on the back and fishing for us under the table.

"I think the Hendersons will take good care of her," I reply.

I help Rain out of the truck and lead her along the walk to the door of Happy Tails. Rain starts to shake, which makes me believe that she remembers Happy Tails and that she isn't happy to be back here. Beyond that, I don't know what she's feeling.

Mrs. Caporale is waiting for Uncle Weldon and Rain and me at the door. She puts her arm across my shoulder. "You're making four people very happy, Rose," she says. "What you're doing is honorable and brave."

Everyone calls me brave. Is this what bravery feels like?

"Come into my office," Mrs. Caporale continues. "The Hendersons are there."

I look up at my uncle and he offers me a smile. Then he puts his hand on my back and we follow Mrs. Caporale through a doorway.

Sitting on chairs in the small office are a man, a woman, a girl who is about my age, and a boy who is probably the prime number age of seven. They're sitting silently. But when they see Rain they all jump to their feet, and then the girl and boy slide onto their knees and throw their arms around Rain.

"Olivia!" the girl cries.

The boy doesn't say anything. He buries his face in Rain's fur.

The woman starts to cry so I don't look at her anymore.

I watch Rain. She sat quietly at first, but now she's standing up and wiggling. Not shaking, wiggling. Every inch of her. She licks the boy's face and then the girl's face. She leaps up against the man's legs. The woman kneels down and Rain puts her paws on her shoulders. She whines in her happy way and then she jumps down and dances back and forth, sticking her snout in the Hendersons' hands.

This is Happy Rain.

And these are happy people, I think. I remember what their house looked like. I try to think about things from the boy's and the girl's perspectives. I decide that they must have been as sad to lose Rain as I was, and that they must feel as happy now as I did on the day Uncle Weldon and I first came to Happy Tails. I think that they still don't have their home, but now they have their dog back.

When Rain stops dancing around and the room grows quieter, Mrs. Caporale brings out some papers for Mr. and Mrs. Henderson. They sign them and then for a moment everyone stands still looking at one another. I drop my eyes to Rain.

Mrs. Henderson crosses the little room and puts her arms around me. I hold very still, my arms at my sides, while she hugs me.

"Thank you, Rose," she says.

"Yes, thank you," says her husband. He looks like maybe he's going to hug me too, but he changes his mind and smiles at me instead.

"Thank you," say the girl and the boy, whose names, I know now, are Jean and Toby.

I think for a moment and then I say, "You're welcome," and I stare at each one of the Hendersons.

Uncle Weldon clears his throat. "Well," he says, "I should get you home, Rose." He turns to the Hendersons. "Would it be possible for Rose to have a few minutes alone with Rain?"

"Of course," says Mr. Henderson, and everyone leaves the room except for Rain and me.

Rain is sitting on her haunches in the middle of the floor. She's still very excited, and when I sit down next to her she jumps to her feet and puts her face against mine, breathing hard.

"That's your family," I say finally. "You're going to go home with them."

Rain continues to gaze at me.

I wrap (rap) my arms around her and feel her soft fur against my cheek. "I love you," I tell her.

Rain leans into me and we sit that way until I hear a knock on the door.

"Rose?" calls Uncle Weldon. "We need to leave now. So do the Hendersons. Have you said good-bye?"

"Yes."

I stand up and lead Rain through the door. She sees the Hendersons and runs to them.

They call good-bye and say thank you to me several more times. I stand at the window in Happy Tails and watch Rain climb into the Hendersons' car. Then I watch the car pull out of the lot and turn onto the drive. I can see Rain's head in the window, her long proud snout, and her pink nose that is the exact color of an eraser. Jean Henderson leans over and whispers in Rain's ear, and Rain cocks her head to the side.

The car turns a corner and Rain disappears.

V

The Last Part

45

The Quiet House

The bulletin board in our classroom changes to SPRING IS COMING!

The air grows warmer.

My father finishes the bridge and now he can drive our truck over it.

Sam Diamond takes his car back.

The afternoons at my house are quiet. My father says he is out looking for work.

When I am at home alone I study my list of homonyms. I look through my mother's box.

That is all.

There is an ache inside of me, a pain.

Is this what bravery feels like? Or loneliness?

Maybe this is an ache of sadness.

46

My Father Has an Argument with His Brother

On a day when the grass in our yard is more green than brown, and the air is warm and smells sweet, and the branches on the trees are fuzzy with new leaves, Uncle Weldon drives me home from Hatford Elementary. He drives across the finished bridge and parks the truck.

My father is standing at the front of his own truck, tinkering with things under the hood. He hasn't been back to the J & R Garage since the day Jerry frickin' fired him. He works on his truck and in the yard now that the bridge is finished. I do not think his job search is going well.

One afternoon last week when Uncle Weldon was driving me home I said, "I guess my father could drive me to school and back now. He still doesn't have a job."

Uncle Weldon started shaking his head before I even finished speaking. "Let's not mention that," he replied.

That's what I was hoping he would say. "Okay."

We rode for a little while longer and then I said, "From my father's perspective, I don't think he wants to run into Mrs. Kushel or Mrs. Leibler. Seeing them once a month is enough for him."

"I think you're exactly right."

Now on this spring day I climb out of the truck. Then Uncle Weldon climbs out of the truck. This is unusual.

"Hey, Wes," my uncle says.

My father steps away from the hood and straightens up. He wipes his hands on a rag that is hanging out of one pocket. "Hey."

"Do you have a minute?" asks Uncle Weldon.

"I guess." My father looks wary.

"Well, I've been thinking. Rose here . . . Rose here should have another dog. Don't you agree?"

I take a step backward. "I didn't say that!" I tell my father.

"Nope," says Uncle Weldon calmly. "This is all my idea."

My father snorts. "*Rose here* didn't appreciate the dog she had, the one I got her. She gave it back. She gave it back when she could have kept it."

Rain is a she, not an it. My father is angry.

"Rain wasn't her dog," my uncle replies.

"She could have kept it," my father repeats. "She didn't have to go looking for the owners."

Uncle Weldon clenches his jaw.

I take another step backward.

"I was just trying to do something nice for her," says my father. "I got her a dog and she gave it back. The one great thing I did. The one great thing."

"Look, Wesley."

"Not another word. I mean it. Not another word."

When my father says "not another word," he does mean it.

Uncle Weldon retreats to his truck, opens the front door, and slides behind the wheel.

"Just think about it. Rose has so lit—" He catches himself. "It's lonely for her. I mean, when you aren't around."

"Rose is fine. She has all she needs here. She's just fine."

"But a dog—"

"You think you know best? You don't know best." My father slaps his hands on the side of his truck.

Uncle Weldon sits motionless behind the wheel.

My mind is whirling. I try to send a message to my uncle. *Please don't say another word. Not another word.* If my father forbids Uncle Weldon to see me, then I will have nothing left.

My uncle opens his mouth. "Are you sure *you* know what's best for Rose?" he asks quietly.

My father pulls a wrench out of his pocket. He aims it at the windshield of Uncle Weldon's truck, but then he lowers his arm to his side. He puts the wrench back in his pocket, shakes his head once, and gets to work under the hood again. His hands are trembling.

Uncle Weldon puts his truck in reverse and begins to turn around. He waves to me through the window, and I give him a small wave back.

Then I run to my bedroom and close the door.

47

In the Middle
of the Night

On nights when I have trouble falling asleep, I lie very still on my back and pick a number. The more awake I am, the higher the number I choose. Then I silently count backwards by three.

One warm night when rain is dripping softly off the roof of the house, I have been lying in bed for nearly an hour and a half and I am still not at all sleepy. I think about school. I think about Rain. I think about Parvani, who now tells me every time she finds new homonyms. I think about Rain some more.

Sleep will not come.

Four hundred ninety-five, 492, 489, 486, 483. I am in the 350s when I start to make mistakes. Finally I feel floaty and drift to sleep.

BANG! The door to my room flies open and in the doorway I see the shape of my father silhouetted by light from the living room.

I look at my clock. I have been asleep for less than twenty minutes.

My father flicks on my light. "I'm taking you to Weldon's," he announces. "Right now."

I raise myself up on my elbows. The time on my clock is 12:02. Why is my father up and dressed at this hour? He hasn't been to The Luck of the Irish tonight.

"What?" I say, but my father is already crossing the living room. I hear the front door open.

I think about what he just said. "I'm taking you to Weldon's." Not "We're going to Weldon's," but "I'm taking you to Weldon's." This sounds like I'm the only one going to my uncle's house. It sounds like I might stay there for a while.

I hurry into the kitchen and grab a garbage bag from under the sink. I hear banging noises outside, as if objects are being thrown into the back of the truck. I whisk the bag into my room and stuff clothes into it, as many as I can grab quickly. I set my backpack next to the garbage bag. I make sure my homonyms list is in the backpack. I'm sliding my mother's box off the shelf in the coat closet when I hear my father shout, "Rose! Get out here right now."

I scramble into the truck with the garbage bag, the backpack, and my mother's box. My father is hurtling down the driveway before I have even closed my door. I'm still fastening my seat belt as we fly across the bridge and start down Hud Road. In the back of the truck things slide from side to side, bags, a suitcase, a cardboard box.

"Why are we going to Uncle Weldon's?" I ask.

My father doesn't answer. He's peering ahead through the windshield at the rain, which is falling harder now. His face is like stone, not soft and slack like when he's been drinking. He doesn't turn to look at me. He drives straight and sure and carefully.

"Why are we going to Uncle Weldon's?" I ask again.

Once in music class, our teacher showed us a tuning fork. He struck it on the edge of a desk and let us take turns putting our hands on it to feel the vibrations. The air in the truck now is like the tuning fork, vibrating. It continues to vibrate after I ask my question the second time and still get no answer.

We ride in silence in the charged atmosphere, through

the dark streets of Hatford, our headlights shining on the falling rain, the slick trees, and once, the eyes of a raccoon hesitating at the side of the road.

"Does Uncle Weldon know I'm coming?" I ask as we turn into his driveway.

My father brings the truck to a halt, but doesn't turn the engine off. He reaches across me and opens my door. "Go now," he says. Then he does something he hasn't done in a long time. He gives me a hug, a quick hug. When his cheek rests against mine I can feel wetness. He turns and faces front, his jaw working.

I climb out of the truck and pull my things after me. I run through the rain to Uncle Weldon's front porch. By the time I turn around, the taillights of the truck are disappearing down the drive.

I ring my uncle's bell. I ring it again and again. The porch light comes on and I see Uncle Weldon's face in the window by the door. One second later the door is flung wide-open.

"Rose!" he exclaims. "What on earth?"

I step toward him. "My father is gone," I say.

48

What Happened to My Mother

Uncle Weldon and I sit on his front porch on a day that seems too hot for early June. There are still two more weeks of school, and every morning Mrs. Kushel opens the windows in our classroom wide, even though bees and flies come in and hum around our heads all day long.

I jiggle my feet up and down and watch a hummingbird hover by a geranium plant.

It's Saturday morning. Uncle Weldon has just said, "Let's put on our thinking caps."

I glance at him. "Why?"

"We need to figure out what to bring to your school party."

We are going to have a party in Mrs. Kushel's room to celebrate the last day of school.

"Cookies?" I suggest. "Chocolate chip cookies?"

Uncle Weldon smiles. "Good idea. We'll go to the store next week and buy the ingredients."

We fall silent again. Sometimes Uncle Weldon and I just sit quietly for long periods of time. We like that. Sitting and thinking.

Every evening we make dinner together and every morning we talk about homonyms. On the weekends we go for rides in his truck—to the state park, to the museum in Ashford, to an outdoor music festival. When we were at the festival, we spread a blanket on the ground and lay on our backs, listening to an orchestra.

"Try to pick out the sounds each instrument makes," Uncle Weldon said. "Listen for the violin, listen for the trombone, listen for the clarinet."

The notes soared into the sky, up to the stars.

On this hot June morning, the hummingbird darting from one flower to another, I suddenly say, "Uncle Weldon, from my mother's perspective, when she went away, why do you think she left her memories behind?"

Uncle Weldon cocks his head at me the way Rain used to do. "What do you mean?" he asks.

I tell him about the box. "She left all her Rose things behind. Why didn't she take them with her? Didn't she want to remember me?"

Now my uncle frowns. "Rose," he says, "do you think your mother walked away from you and your dad? Is that what your father told you?"

"Yes. Yes," I say, since my uncle has asked me two questions in a row.

Uncle Weldon's face is soft and gentle. He reaches a hand toward me, touches my knee, pulls his hand back. "Your mother didn't leave," he says. "She died. When you were very young."

"She's dead?"

"Yes."

"How did she die?"

"She had an aneurysm in her heart. She died very quickly."

"Why did my father tell me she left us?"

Uncle Weldon shakes his head. He sips his coffee. "Maybe he was trying to shield you. Maybe he thought you would be too sad if you knew she had died."

"But he let me think she *left* us. I thought she left because of me."

Uncle Weldon touches my knee again, which is all right. It's just a little touch. "Your father didn't always make smart choices," he says, "but he did try to do right by you."

"Is that why *he* left?"

My uncle looks at the hummingbird. He shakes his head again. "I don't know. We didn't talk about it, your father and I, but I think he thought you'd be better off with me."

"Was it hard for him to leave?"

"Yes, I think it was."

So my father and I have something else in common. We are both brave.

49

Hud Road

That summer is one of the hottest anyone can remember. Uncle Weldon buys a big wooden swing that we paint green before hanging it on the front porch. We sit on it every evening while we wait for the air to cool, Uncle Weldon rocking us lazily back and forth, back and forth, his foot pushing off from the geranium pot. We sit on the swing most mornings too, even weekday mornings before we leave for Uncle Weldon's day at work and my day at a program called Summertime Academy, where I meet other kids with the official diagnosis of high-functioning autism.

One Sunday morning we're on the swing and I'm looking across a dusty golden field and through some trees to a road that, if you followed it for 2.3 miles, would lead to Hud. Uncle Weldon and I visited my old house several days ago. We looked through the windows at the empty rooms. Uncle Weldon ran his hand thoughtfully over the foreclosure notice tacked to the front door. We haven't heard from my father since the night he left me with Uncle Weldon, so we were the ones who cleared the house out last month. I didn't want to keep anything except Rain's belongings— her leash and bowl and toys. I put them in a bag under my bed.

We are just swinging quietly on this Sunday when Uncle Weldon says to me, "When should we visit Happy Tails again?"

I glance at him. "Well . . ."

"Don't you think it's time for another visit? There are probably some new dogs up for adoption."

"I don't know."

"Come on." Uncle Weldon smiles at me. "Just another look? A little peek? Wouldn't it be nice to sit out here with a dog between us?"

"A dog on a swing?" Now I smile. "Maybe we could go next weekend."

Uncle Weldon holds out his hand and I shake it.

We have made a deal.

"I thought of a new homonym last night," I say. "It's a good one: 'weighed' and 'wade.' "

"That *is* a good one," my uncle agrees. "Was there room on your list?"

"Yes. You know who else has a homonyms list now?"

"No. Who?"

"Parvani. I'm going to call her and tell her about 'weighed' and 'wade.' "

Uncle Weldon brings the swing to a stop and we cross our fingers and touch our hearts.

I look across the field again and then up to the sky, which is a vast pale blue. I remember the music festival, and the notes that soared above our heads. I think about the homonyms *soared* and *sword*. They're an interesting pair, because *soared* is a very nice word, especially when you imagine musical notes swooshing through the evening air, but *sword* indicates weaponry, so that isn't a nice word at all. That's one of the many things I like about homonyms. Most of them seem unrelated, some seem to be opposites, like *soared* and *sword*, but a few make lovely connections if you're open to changing your perspective when you think about them.

I stand up, then squint my eyes shut for (fore/four) a

moment, remembering the night (knight) with Uncle Weldon when the music soared (sword) through (threw) the air (heir/err), and the notes and the sky and our (hour) hearts were one (won).

Author's Note

The tale of Rose and Rain began in 2011 after Hurricane Irene swept up the East Coast of the United States and made an unexpected inland turn. After the storm I walked along my road in upstate New York, day after day, watching as downed trees were cleared from yards, roofs were reshingled, and washed-out bridges and stone walls were rebuilt. My dog, Sadie, was at my side and I thought about pets who had become separated from their owners during the storm. I began to spin a tale about a lost dog.

At the same time, Rose began to make her presence known to me. She was a young girl on the Autism Spectrum; a girl who's verbal and bright and whose dog is the center of her baffling and sometimes unpleasant world. Slowly the elements of the story—Rose, Rain, and the storm—came together.

Writing can be a solitary business, but most stories

are a group effort. Many thanks to my editors, Liz Szabla and Jean Feiwel, for their insights, their patience, and their faith, and for encouraging me to dig deeper. And thank you to my friend Jamey Wolff, cofounder and Program Director of the Center for Spectrum Services in New York's Hudson Valley. The Center serves students on the Autism Spectrum. Jamey graciously allowed me to spend a morning at the school in Kingston, talking with students, observing the interaction between students and teachers, and asking Jamey question after question. When the rough draft of the story was finished, Jamey was one of the first to read it. Her help was invaluable.

Finally, thank you to sweet Sadie, who introduced me to the world of dogs, and whose behavior I observed every day of her fifteen years. She was by my side as I wrote the story, and was a daily inspiration.

Thank you for reading this FEIWEL AND FRIENDS book.
The Friends who made

RAIN REIGN

possible are:

Jean Feiwel	publisher
Liz Szabla	editor in chief
Rich Deas	senior creative director
Holly West	associate editor
Dave Barrett	executive managing editor
Nicole Liebowitz Moulaison	production manager
LAUREN A. BURNIAC	editor
Anna Roberto	associate editor
Christine Barcellona	administrative assistant

FOLLOW US ON FACEBOOK
OR VISIT US ONLINE AT
MACKIDS.COM.

OUR BOOKS ARE
FRIENDS FOR LIFE